AINSLEY KEATON

The Beachfront Girls

BOOKS

By Ainsley Keaton

Sconset Beach

Vinci Books

vinci-books.com

Published by Vinci Books Ltd in 2025

1

Copyright © Ainsley Keaton 2022

Paperback ISBN: 9781036703745

Chapter One

Sarah

Sarah had moved into her new home on Miacomet Beach and, having gotten the proper permits for all the renovations that she wanted, made her small home as shiny as the penny that had enabled her to buy this home in the first place. She was lucky that she got a compliant board who heard her permit requests because her home was built in the 1800s, therefore it was considered to be historic, and Nantucket was notorious for not allowing interior renovations in many of the historic homes.

But Sarah managed to get permits to do everything she wanted to do, which included raising the ceilings and knocking out walls so that the home, which had been decorated in early 1970s shag carpeting, combined with 1950s black-and-white checked tiles in the bathrooms, now was completely sleek and modern. It now had an open floor concept, with hardwood floors throughout, modern light fixtures, and a completely remodeled kitchen that featured an island, granite countertops, and even granite floor tiles in grainy black.

The ladies had helped, of course, and so did Deacon, whose job was contracting. Sarah paid all of them over their objections, and she paid Deacon's going rate, even though he, too, objected. But they were invaluable in getting her house together. They cheerfully brought over bottles of wine that they drank while they painted walls and helped her move in furniture she had just bought for the place.

When she left Monterey, she had very little to her name. Her dog, Bella, and souvenirs from around the world were all that she packed in her SUV because that's all she had in the world. She had been a longtime companion for a very wealthy man, and her life was reduced to whatever could fit into the trunk of her SUV. So, when she bought this house, she didn't have much of her own, but she had a ball shopping for couches, end tables, coffee tables, beds, light fixtures, bookshelves, desks, knickknacks, pictures, and just everything that was going to make her house a home.

Now, as she walked around her house with the cherry hardwood floors, the leather couches, the funky lamps, the flatscreen television, and a few vintage pieces - such as the real record player that she picked up at a thrift store that she filled with secondhand records that she bought at a vintage record store in Boston - Sarah felt an overwhelming sense of happiness.

This was her place. Perhaps for the first time in her life, she was living in a place that was only hers. It didn't belong to a billionaire who kept her in the manner he desired, and she wasn't sharing it with a roommate or her mother. This place was hers, and that meant the world to her.

Sarah was experiencing a bit of downtime in her

schedule because it was still early spring. Ava, the sister who employed her, still had plenty of vacancies in her bed and breakfast, and her dining room was only about 25% full, so Ava did not want to have Sarah on full-time in her role as a sommelier. When Ava's business inevitably picked up after Memorial Day, and she once again had a full house and waiting lists, Sarah would return to working full-time for Ava as a sommelier and all-around utility help. Whether she was chopping vegetables, taking reservations, or helping to clean the rooms, Sarah was there for Ava for whatever she needed.

But, as it was only March, there wasn't a whole lot for Sarah to do. She was going to possibly try to find a job as a waitress in one of the restaurants, or a bartender position, but the sale of a very rare penny that was sent to her by Olivia, her deceased boyfriend Noland's wife, fetched almost $3 million and changed her life. Now she had money in the bank, a paid-for house, and getting a job during the off-season was no longer a requirement.

So, she was looking for something to do. And that something was looking after young Emerson, the daughter of her friend Quinn. Quinn was working 60 hours a week in her interior design business, and Emerson needed somebody to be there for her when she got home from school. So, that somebody was Sarah. She was delighted to watch the young girl because Emerson was wickedly intelligent, irreverent, and quite funny.

And so it was that Sarah found out about Emerson's new cause. Emerson was a very talented violinist, and she practiced the violin quite often. She didn't have to do a lot of homework or studying because she was just naturally a gifted student who got straight A's without even trying. And Emerson's mind was always moving at lightning speed.

Sarah sometimes had difficulty keeping up with her, but Emerson entertained her.

One day, Emerson came home and slammed down her backpack. "Dude," she said with a raise of her eyebrow. "You won't believe what my school is doing."

When Emerson came home, Sarah was sitting on the couch, reading a copy of *Architectural Digest.* She was an architect by training and constantly missed her old profession. She was considering renewing her architectural license, although that prospect seemed overwhelming. "What is your school doing?"

Emerson rolled her eyes and flopped down on the couch next to Sarah. "They're like talking about banning books, dude. We're talking things like *Huckleberry Finn, The Great Gatsby, Gone With the Wind, To Kill a Mockingbird, Catcher in the Rye, Beloved* and *1984.*"

Sarah narrowed her eyes at her young charge. "Oh my God. Sounds like the censorship police have descended upon Nantucket. It had to happen sooner or later, huh?"

"Yeah. I'm organizing a group at my school to protest this. It's some of the same kids I've gotten organized to petition the United States government to ban assault weapons and open more family planning clinics."

Emerson had managed to find, in her fairly liberal school, young progressives who were agitating for real change. The group put their words into action, and this action consisted of letter writing, petitions, organizing marches, and creating Tik Tok campaigns aimed at getting people to register to vote. Emerson also phone banked at the local Democratic headquarters once or twice a month. The teen was very interested in gun safety, family planning, climate change, and just about any issue that especially affected her generation.

And now, apparently, Emerson was also interested in censorship issues.

Sarah was amazed at the teen's energy, and the young girl inspired her. Sarah never really got into activism when she was young, although she knew her mother was active in causes.

"When is the next school board meeting?" Sarah asked. "I'd like to go and give them hell in person." Sarah had read almost all of the books that Emerson said would possibly be banned, and while all of them had disturbing elements, she didn't believe any of them should cease to be available to students who wanted to read them.

Emerson raised an eyebrow and smiled. "Aunt Sarah, I want you to go to that next school board meeting, which is next Thursday evening. But I think you should also run for school board. I think you would be perfect for it, and you don't have a whole lot going on right now. So you have the time for it."

Sarah smiled. "We'll see about that. In the meantime, though, I want to attend that school board meeting. You say it's next Thursday evening. At what time?"

"6 o'clock."

———————————

And so Sarah found herself going to the school board meeting of Emerson's school, which was called Thomas Jefferson Middle School. The issue of the book banning was one that apparently attracted a lot of people because the room was filled to capacity. The ten school board members were sitting at the front of the room, behind long tables, and most looked like they were girded for battle.

The school board members called the meeting to order,

reviewed some of the measures they proposed for the school, and then opened the floor for questions or comments.

One by one, concerned adults stood up to address their issues with the school. One parent complained that the school needed more after-school programs that were interesting to a wide variety of students because her young daughter was not interested in anything the school offered. Others had issues with other school policies. A few objected to the censorship issue, but there were others who were supportive. Sarah carefully listened to the arguments and made notes. She understood there were two sides, and she was determined to portray her side to the best of her ability.

Finally, it was time for her to speak to the school board. She stood up and cleared her throat. "I, for one, don't believe any books should be banned. Well, strike that. Obviously, books that are just sheerly pornographic and have no value to a young mind should be banned. But the books we're talking about are classics. And they deal with themes that our children will have to deal with sooner or later. They don't glamorize racism or suicide or murder - they're cautionary tales. For instance, *The Great Gatsby* is on the list to be banned because Gatsby and Daisy have an affair, but Gatsby ends up murdered, so how is that glamorizing extramarital sex? And for another instance, *1984* is a book that goes into the horrors of fascism. It doesn't glorify anything. And we need more books that deal with slavery and racism, not less. Everybody needs to be exposed to these realities of life, and the best way to expose our kids to things they might find repugnant is through art and literature. Young minds can be molded by art and literature, which is why Nazis were so anxious to ban anything that didn't hew to their ideology."

Then Sarah sat down, and a man stood up. He was a good-looking guy, dressed in khakis and a light blue button-down, his dark hair cut short on the sides and long on top, with large green eyes that were currently flashing anger in Sarah's direction.

"I'm so sorry, Ms. Flynn, but the moment you start talking about Nazis, you lose me," he said. "Banning these books is not the first step towards Nazism or fascism. It's simply protecting our young children from concepts they're not ready for. I don't want my 13-year-old daughter to have access to a book where a mother kills her child, a young boy drops an F-bomb every other word, or the N-word is used flagrantly. Many kids can handle these themes, but many can't."

Sarah made a face at the guy. And then she opened her mouth to defend herself, but this guy wasn't finished. "And, Miss Flynn, I understand you don't have a kid here at this school. I don't think you have a dog in this fight."

How dare he? Just because she was childless meant she didn't have a say in how young people were educated? Her childless status meant she couldn't care about the future of the nation's youth? Even if she didn't have young Emerson in her care five days a week for a couple of hours every day, she still would care about issues that affected young people. They were the future, and they were the ones who would have to live with bad decisions that adults made for them. And they didn't have a say.

Sarah stood up again. "I'm sorry, I didn't get your name," she said to the arrogant man who was still glowering at her.

"Max Stein," the guy said. "My daughter Julia is an 8th grader here at this school, and she read the book *Beloved*. She's been having nightmares about it ever since."

"Well, Mr. Stein, I resent you implying that just because I don't have a child, I don't have a say. I'm here to represent my young charge, who also is in the eighth grade and wants to have access to all the books that expand her mind. She understands, unlike you, that learning about scary ideas when you're young builds understanding of complex topics that will affect her life, and the lives of her peers, for generations to come. And, with all due respect, if an individual parent doesn't want their child reading a certain book, the answer is simple – that parent needs to tell the kid they can't have that book. The answer is not to say that no other kids can have access to it."

As Sarah sat down, half the room started to cheer for her, which was mixed in with a smattering of boos. She crossed her arms and glared at the guy. And while one person after another stood up and spoke, Sarah continued to glare at Mr. Stein. He just had such a smug look on his face, like he had all the answers for everybody. And if there was one thing that Sarah hated in life, it was a guy who thought he knew everything. Like this Max Stein apparently thought.

She wished she had at least one of her ladies there, if only because she wanted someone to rant to about the guy who dressed her down in front of everybody.

And after the meeting, Sarah knew one thing – she would run for school board. If only because she wanted to lord it over arrogant jerks like Max Stein.

Chapter Two

Ava

Ava was admiring her garden and the daffodils that were just starting to peek through the ground after having gone dormant since the previous summer when Sarah marched into Ava's house.

"Hey, girlie, what's going on?" Ava asked Sarah.

Sarah shook her head. "You won't believe the kind of arrogant jerk I met last night. You remember I went to Emerson's school last night to address the board about them banning some books, right?"

Ava nodded her head. Sarah had told Ava about her plans to run for the school board at Emerson's school, and Ava thought it was a pretty good idea. After all, nine months out of the year, Sarah didn't have much to do in her life. She worried about her sister. While Sarah never said as much, Ava thought that maybe her beautiful sister was a little bit lonely. Yes, Sarah had her friends there on Nantucket, and during the summer months, she was busy helping out there at the 'Sconset Inn. But, during the lean months, Sarah didn't have much going on, and Ava worried her sister would get bored.

So, her running for school board would be a good way to get active in the community and give her something constructive to do.

"Right, I remember," Ava said.

"Well, there was a guy there last night who had the nerve to imply that because I didn't have a kid in school, I didn't have a right to say anything about the school board's proposal to ban a bunch of classics."

Ava knew that the fact that she didn't have any children was a sore spot for her sister. It wasn't her decision not to have children. It was her ex-boyfriend Nolan's decision. Nolan lived to travel around the world for several months out of the year, so having children would, in his view, have been out of the question. While Ava understood the reasoning behind his decision that the two of them wouldn't have kids - it would be difficult to travel with children - Ava also knew that that decision broke Sarah's heart.

That was a regret Sarah carried around with her. Her sister wanted to leave the man 20 years ago or so because he did something unforgivable to her, but she didn't. She was railroaded into pleading guilty to a drug charge that she had nothing to do with. Nolan didn't help her fight the charge or the revocation of her architectural license. In fact, he wrote letters to the architectural board that damned her regarding the drug charge and lied and said she dealt drugs to children. He did these heinous acts because he wanted to control her. He knew that if she had a felony record and no architectural license, she would have no choice but to stay with him.

And so, even though she wanted to leave and find a life

of her own, she stayed. And that decision cost her her dream of having children of her own. So this guy standing up and dressing Sarah down by telling her she didn't have a say at the school board meeting because she didn't have children probably hit her where it hurt the most.

Ava put her hand on Sarah's shoulder. "Don't let it get to you, babe," she said. "You have a right to speak up. Emerson is a student of that school. Besides, the school board's decisions affects everybody in the community. If it affects our children, it affects us. So, you just speak your piece and don't worry about what others have to say."

Sarah just nodded her head. "I shouldn't let it bother me, but it does. It happened last night, and I'm still stewing about it. I don't know why I'm letting it get to me so much. Maybe it's because what he said was so hurtful or because he was so rude about it. I mean, who does he think he is? And he was just so smug about it. So arrogant."

Sarah shook her head.

"Hey, I know you're excited about getting involved with the school board. Just don't let that jerk get you down."

Ava never knew Sarah had any kind of doubt in her life. Her sister was always so confident. In high school, she was the queen, the beautiful girl everybody wanted to be around. Girls wanted to be her, and boys wanted to date her. Everybody just always flocked around her.

It was the same thing in college. In college, Sarah was a member of the Delta Gamma sorority, the best house on campus. There, as in high school, Sarah enjoyed immense popularity. Whenever Ava visited her on campus, she always had social events to go to. Parties, dances, gathering with friends – Sarah always had something going on because people always wanted her around.

But something happened along the way. Sarah lost her

special glow. Ava couldn't help but think that Nolan had much to do with that. He beat her down, probably because he recognized her special light that attracted so many people. The only way he could control her would be to extinguish that light. So, while Sarah seemed perfectly happy there on the island, there was also a kind of sadness about her. A regret that her life didn't quite turn out the way she had hoped it would.

And now, another man seemed to recognize Sarah's light and wanted to dim that light, at the very least. And Sarah needed some kind of moral support from her friends so she could pursue this school board position, which might go a long way toward giving Sarah back the confidence she always had when she was young.

Sarah said nothing but just looked around the garden. "It looks like the daffodils will be coming up pretty soon," she said. "Maybe if I don't get this school board thing, I can take up gardening. I've always wanted to learn more about it, but Nolan hired a team of gardeners to take care of our grounds. And, when I wanted to learn more about growing plants and flowers, he told me not to bother with it. But I just might bother with it now. After all, I have my own back-yard, and I'll need to plant some flowers to make it spectacular."

Ava furrowed her brows. There was definitely something going on with her sister. Sarah was just looking around the garden with a sad expression.

"What's going on?" Ava asked Sarah.

Sarah just shrugged her shoulders. "It's just hurtful. Sometimes I wonder what my role is in life. I guess it's just a hangover from feeling for so many years that I was useless. That's how Nolan made me feel. He made me believe I wasn't good for anything. And now I finally have latched onto something I hope will give me some kind of pride in my life, and this Max guy threw cold water on it. Now I feel like I shouldn't run for school board. Because he's right – I don't have a kid in that school. I don't have a kid in any school. I guess it's really not my business what happens."

"Sarah, you felt such a sense of pride when you got your certification to become a sommelier. And you're an excellent sommelier. You're very knowledgeable, and you're so helpful to me. You've stocked my wine cellar with some of the best wines worldwide. You have a passion for it and a talent. You're not useless."

Sarah smiled, but Ava could tell that it wasn't a genuine smile. "I know. It's just that I don't have an outlet for my wine talents during the off-season. I don't know, I'm feeling sorry for myself. And I can't let other people's words hurt me so much."

Ava put her arm around her sister. "Sarah, you need to find the young girl who was so confident that she ruled the school. And you definitely need to go forward with your plan to run for school board. You have a very focused vision for how you want the kids in Emerson's school to be. You've talked so much to Emerson about what she thinks is wrong with her school, and that young girl wants your help. Her own mother can't take the time to run for school board or even go to school board meetings, so you have to go in Quinn's stead. Think of Emerson as your child, too. In fact, Emerson is kind of all of our child. It takes a village to raise a child. That village is me, you, and Hallie, along with Quinn."

"So, I guess I'm part of Emerson's village, which means I have a dog in the fight. Is that what you're saying?" Sarah asked her.

"That's what I'm saying."

Sarah took a deep breath, and then the doorbell rang.

Ava shrugged her shoulders. "I wasn't expecting anybody to check in today, but maybe it's a walk-in. Let me check who's there, and as soon as I get them taken care of, we can devise a game plan for you. Because I really want you to pursue the school board thing."

"Okay."

Ava walked to the door and opened it up.

And almost fainted dead away.

Her ex-husband, Christopher, was standing on her porch.

Chapter Three

Ava

Christopher was there on her porch. The man who stole all her money and then hightailed it to parts unknown, leaving her in the lurch, causing a wave of panic she never got over. It's hard to get over the sense of betrayal you feel when a man does that to you.

"What are you doing here?" Ava asked him. "Seriously, you have a lot of nerve coming around here, showing your face."

To her surprise, Christopher looked embarrassed, chastened. "I need to talk to you. And, before you slam the door in my face, I need you to check your bank account. You'll see I put all the money I took from you, plus+50% interest."

Ava looked at Christopher like he had grown another head. What was he talking about? How did he just suddenly get that kind of money? It would be understating the matter to say that Ava was suspicious about all of it.

Sarah came to the door. She looked at Ava, then at

Christopher, and gave Ava a questioning look. Sarah had never met Christopher, so she obviously didn't know him from Adam. But she did shoot Ava a look of concern.

"Sarah, I don't want to be rude, but why don't you go up to the deck or the sunroom and wait for me? I still want to talk to you about the school board issue, but I must deal with something first."

Sarah just nodded her head and disappeared back into the house.

Ava faced Christopher. "So what did you do, just Venmo $1.5 million to me?" Ava asked.

Christopher shook his head. "No. I guess I wasn't clear. I opened an account in your name, only in your name, and that account has $1.5 million in it." Then he handed her some paperwork about the bank account he had opened. "Go ahead, check it. You'll see what I did."

Ava narrowed her eyes. "I want nothing from you. Let's just make that perfectly clear. I mean, obviously, I'm not going to give the money back to you if you opened up a bank account in my name with that kind of money. You owe me much more than that because of the mental distress you put me through. I should send you my therapist bills. So, I'll check this bank account out and make sure it's solid, but don't think I'll ever forget what you did because I won't. I can't forget, and I can't forgive."

Christopher hung his head. "I thought you'd say that. At any rate, I'm happy I finally did the right thing for you. I had a hard time waking up every day and looking in the mirror, seeing the man I had become. Hitting rock bottom doesn't even start to describe how I've been feeling about doing that to you. But now my conscience is clear."

"Is it really clear? How could it possibly be? You didn't just steal all that money from me, but you left me in the lurch. Just left without even a note. I can't imagine what got into you, and I certainly can't imagine what kind of excuse you'll come up with. All I know is that I've moved on, there's a new kind and thoughtful man in my life, and I want nothing to do with you."

Christopher nodded his head. "I didn't expect the red carpet to be laid out for me. To say the least. But I was hoping that you would at least hear me out."

Just then, Jessica, Ava's all-around assistant and surrogate daughter, came down the stairs with a vacuum in her hand. "Hey," she said and then took a look at Christopher and stopped. There was a look of recognition in her crystalline blue eyes when she saw him. And then she looked right back at Ava. "I got all the rooms spick-and-span," she said. "I was wondering if I could take a break? I'm supposed to have lunch with Andrew today. He'll be leaving pretty soon for Los Angeles."

Jessica had come to Ava last summer. When Jessica arrived on Ava's doorstep, the young lady had been suffering from an addiction to OxyContin. However, she had quit before asking Ava if she could stay at her inn in exchange for helping around the house. She met Andrew, who was an internationally popular singer-songwriter who also was staying with Ava for the summer. Jessica discovered the root of her trauma went back to when she was four years old and her mother was murdered in front of her. Since then, she had been in therapy and got in the water as much as possible – scuba diving, sailing with Andrew, surfing with Andrew, and swimming – which also was healing for her. And she had really come a long way in her recovery.

As it happened, Andrew was related to Jessica's trauma. It was his father who shot her mother on Jessica's fifth birthday. Her mother stepped in front of the bullet that was meant for Andrew. Jessica had blocked all of that out for all those years, which was the root cause of her addiction.

Jessica still went to AA several times a week. She had explained to Ava that she loved the people she met during these meetings. They had become like family to her and kept her on track as far as not going back to her painkiller addiction. She loved them because they all had the same issue as her, and it meant a lot to her to know people who struggled the same way she did.

Ava was distracted by Christopher. So she halfheartedly told Jessica to go and have lunch with Andrew. "Have fun," Ava said, only half thinking about Jessica.

Jessica nodded her head. Ava looked at Christopher and saw that he had the same look of recognition on his face when he looked at Jessica.

It was obvious these two knew each other, but how?

Jessica left. Christopher watched her leave but didn't say a word to Ava about how he knew her.

So Ava decided to go ahead and ask him. "What was that?" she asked him.

"What was what?" Christopher volleyed back.

"You know Jessica. That was obvious from both of your faces. What gives?"

Christopher just shook his head. "I don't know what you're talking about. Anyhow, I wanted you to know I've made good on the money I took from you. I wasn't expecting you to forgive me, so I'm not disappointed that I'll walk away from this house empty-handed. I only decided to stop by because I wanted to give you the information about the bank account I opened up for you."

Ava just nodded her head. She wouldn't say "thank you" because that would be just too friendly. And the last thing she wanted was to be friendly to the man who betrayed her so completely. "Okay. You told me about the bank account and dropped off the information about it. And, if you would excuse me, I have a lot of work to do."

That was a lie. Ava's bed-and-breakfast was only 25% full, and Jessica worked for her, so Ava didn't have many responsibilities. Truth be told, the only thing she had going on that day was getting caught up on a book she was reading. But she couldn't stand the sight of Christopher in front of her, so she wanted him to hightail it the hell out of there.

Christopher just nodded his head. "Okay. But I wanted to let you know that I'll be staying on the island for a little while. You know, just in case you run into me at the farmers market or something like that. I don't want you to think I'm stalking you or anything like that."

Ava narrowed her eyes. "What do you mean, you're going to be staying on the island for a while? Why?"

Oh, this was lovely. Just lovely. Nantucket was an island that was only 14 miles long and 3 miles wide. During the off-season, which it currently was, it being only March, only about 10,000 people lived here. There was a good chance that Ava would run into anyone on the island on any given day. And one of those 10,000 people on this tiny island would be Christopher? Oh, no.

No.

"Christopher, I don't know what your game is. All I can tell you is I'm not playing it. Now, I know that it's your life, and I can't tell you how to live it, and I can't tell you where to live it. What I can tell you is that I was here first. And, quite frankly, this island is not big enough for both of us. I've established a business here and have friends and a boyfriend. I would leave this island to get away from you, but I don't think I should have to. So, I respectfully ask you not to live here on Nantucket."

Christopher took a deep breath. "I'm sorry, I really am. I don't want to live here, but I have to. But I'll try to stay out of your way."

Ava rolled her eyes. "Please do. Please try to stay out of my way. If you see me out on the town, don't acknowledge me. And I won't acknowledge you."

At that, Ava slammed the door in his face.

Ava immediately found Sarah, who was sitting in the sunroom. "Girl, you won't imagine what just happened. But I can tell you that this calls for a bottle of wine. Maybe even two."

Sarah smiled. "You read my mind."

Chapter Four

Ava

Ava invited the ladies over that evening. It was time for another one of their emergency pow-wows that they always had whenever stuff went down. And this situation definitely called for several bottles of wine and some venting with her closest friends.

Sarah was already there, and Quinn came over that evening with Hallie. Quinn was working hard on a billionaire's mansion. She was an interior decorator who was very much in demand on the island and lived in the same neighborhood as Ava. Hallie was a co-owner of a unique spa and metaphysical center and also was building a clientele as a life coach. She owned the spa and metaphysical place with a psychic named Willow. The latter was well trained in acupuncture, crystals, tarot, and sound therapy. Willow also went further in healing rituals. Willow was beautiful and gifted, and Ava thought her son, Jackson, was really into her.

Willow was not at Ava's that night, however. She was apparently busy doing something else, and Ava was disappointed she wasn't there. She wanted Willow's insight on what was going on with Christopher. Because something was going on, obviously. She couldn't imagine any legitimate reason why he would be staying on this tiny island, especially during the off-season. The guy was a high-powered investment banker in New York before he high-tailed it to Europe with all of Ava's money, one step ahead of the loan sharks.

Ava had heard through the grapevine that Christopher ended up living in Paris after he fled the United States. So, he went from New York City to Paris. One huge metropolis to another. Nothing in Christopher's background and desires would ever lead him to stay on a tiny island where nothing much was happening for any length of time. To say that he was just not a small-town type guy would be understating the matter.

So why was he there? Did he just want to torment her?

She told the ladies what happened with Christopher after ordering some sushi delivered to her by Door Dash. She would've invited the ladies to dinner but didn't want to risk running into Christopher.

And she hated the feeling that she would run into him regularly. But she just knew she would. She didn't want to become a hermit because of it. But, at least that evening, she was afraid to leave the house.

Quinn shook her head when she heard the story. "Ava, I don't know what to tell you. That's just the craziest thing I've ever heard."

Quinn knew Christopher, as did Hallie. Both ladies actually really liked Ava's husband. And he was still her husband because she never divorced him. She didn't have the energy to try to track him down to have him served with divorce papers. She had a lot of other things going on – getting fired, inheriting this house, renovating it, running it as a bed-and-breakfast – so she just never got around to it.

Now, he was on Nantucket, and Ava could see a silver lining. Now she could properly divorce him. So, that was one good thing.

"I know," Ava said. "But, I went to the bank where he opened my account. It was Bank of America. I spoke to a personal banker there, and everything checks out. I now have an account in my name with $1.5 million. So, he wasn't lying about that. But I don't even want to think about how he managed to get that money together. I'm not even going to ask."

Hallie grinned. "Maybe he grifted somebody. He probably hit up some rich old lady in the South of France. Married her, and then she died, and now he has the money."

Ava used her chopsticks to pick up a slice of her rainbow roll and stuck the food in her mouth. She served hot sake with the delicious sushi and was getting buzzed. "That would make him a bigamist," Ava said. "I would remind you that we never divorced. But I wouldn't put it past him to marry somebody else while he was still married to me. How would that even work?"

She was a lawyer but not a domestic lawyer, so she was unfamiliar with how bigamists get caught. She supposed it was possible that Christopher, in a foreign country, would have gotten away with marrying somebody for their money. Although she imagined that a decent European lawyer would've done their due diligence to discover that Christopher was already married to her. So, even if he married an old lady who died and left him everything, the only thing that would've happened to him would be that he would've ended up in jail.

Quinn settled back in her chair. "Ava, it's not hard to believe that maybe Christopher came into money somehow. He was an investment banker. He probably went to Europe, got his life together, and made enough money to pay you back with interest."

Ava just raised her eyebrow. "No, there's a story there. Something went on over there. Christopher is probably involved in something illegal, and now I'm the recipient of his ill-gotten gains. I fully expect the FBI to be on my doorstep at any moment, telling me that my new bank account has been frozen because Christopher stole the money to put into it. I'm not going to touch a penny of that money because I don't want to go to prison with him. I'd be receiving stolen property, and they could tell me I was being willfully blind if I tried to tell them that I had no idea the money was stolen."

Sarah just shook her head. "Sis, you're spinning. You have no proof that Christopher stole millions of dollars and gave it to you. Maybe he really is trying to make good with you. Maybe it's just like he said – he couldn't live with himself, so he cleaned up his act, worked really hard, and paid you back. Now he can look at himself in the mirror. Now he can sleep at night. It might be something as simple as that."

Ava took a drink of her sake and another slice of her rainbow roll. This slice of the rainbow roll had salmon on top of the rice, which was Ava's favorite. "I love you, Sarah, but you didn't know the man. And, apparently, I didn't know him either. I mean, I was married to him for twenty years. Yet I don't think I knew him at all, and I still don't know him. I'm still dumbfounded about his actions."

Ava shook her head. She took a deep breath.

"So, what am I going to do? He's going to be on this island. I'm going to see him whenever I go out. I just know that we're going to end up going to the same restaurants, the same stores, the same Farmer's Market."

Quinn made a face. "Why do you care? He's your ex-husband. He betrayed you, and you've long since been over the guy. And you have Deacon. Just go about your life and ignore him. If you see him in the supermarket, hide behind one of the shelves. If you see him in a restaurant, ask the hostess to seat you as far away from him as possible. You don't have to deal with him."

"I know. But it just seems weird he's going to be around. This is a small town, you know. Everyone seems to know everyone around this joint."

Ava sat back in her chair and shook her head. She supposed the ladies were correct. She could avoid him. That would have to be the only option because she couldn't very well tell him that he had to leave. It wasn't her place, and it was a free country.

She was just going to have to live with the fact that anytime she went out of the house, she could very well run into the guy who ruined her life.

Chapter Five

Sarah

One day, not too long after the infamous school board meeting, Sarah hosted Julia Stein. Quinn had to go out of town because she had a family emergency back in her hometown of Helen, Georgia. She would be gone the entire weekend, so Sarah eagerly agreed to watch Emerson while Quinn was gone.

Emerson asked Sarah if she was okay with Julia coming to stay the night, and Sarah said, "the more, the merrier!"

She really enjoyed being around young people. They inspired her with their energy, ideas, and way of viewing the world. She even found herself not minding the music the young people listened to. She wasn't crazy about rap, but she didn't mind some of the Megan Thee Stallion and Cardi B stuff. When she was their age, she listened to The Police, Tears for Fears and Howard Jones, along with all the other great New Wave 80s bands. Sarah was prejudiced in favor of the music of her youth, but she was

open-minded about what the kids of today were listening
to.

Julia arrived that Friday at around 5, and the two girls
went into Emerson's room to do whatever teenage girls did
behind closed doors. Sarah smiled, having been taken back
to the days when she would have a young friend over. In her
day, she and her friends would make silly prank calls, going
down the phone book and calling random people to ask
them if the refrigerator was running. If they said "yes," she
and her giggling friend would tell the unsuspecting victim to
"run after it!" Another fine joke was about asking random
people if they had Prince Albert in a can. If they said "yes,"
Sarah would tell the person to "let him out!" Of course,
today's kids wouldn't even know what a phone book was for,
let alone know how to use one to play dumb pranks.

The early 80s were definitely a more innocent time to be
an adolescent, Sarah mused. It was the days before the
internet, cell phones, social media, ride shares and violent
video games. Computers were lame and ran on the dreaded
DOS system with the green screen. She never heard much
about perverts meeting young girls or sex trafficking in those
days. MTV showed videos back then, and she'd watch the
channel for hours every day. And so did all her friends. The
John Hughes movies that depicted teenage life did so
cleanly and innocently. Whether it was Samantha from *16
Candles* pining after the high school hunk or Ferris Bueller
taking the day off from school to go to the museum and to a
ballgame, the hijinks her film peers engaged in were silly
and clean fun.

Nowadays, she knew that the kids around Emerson and
Julia's age were not nearly as innocent as she was. They
were exposed to disinformation and perverts through social
media. Emerson told her that drugs were rampant around

her school, and kids were having sex at younger and younger ages. Yet she still was inspired by the kids, and especially by children like Emerson, who got involved in so many causes affecting her generation.

The two girls came down for dinner at around 6 o'clock. Quinn told Sarah that Emerson was no longer a picky eater who lived on junk food. So when Sarah brought out the rotisserie chicken, mashed potatoes, and asparagus, she was reasonably sure the two girls would eagerly eat everything up. And she was correct in that, as they sat down and immediately dug into their food while chatting rapidly about everything under the sun.

"I heard you're going to be running for school board," Julia said to Sarah. "You should really hire my dad to manage your campaign. He's managed a lot of D.C. campaigns. Senators and Representatives. Now he manages a lot of local campaigns, but he always wins his races."

Sarah cocked her head. "That sounds interesting. Do you know how much he charges?"

She shrugged her shoulders. "Not sure. I can text him and ask."

Emerson piped up. "I don't think Aunt Sarah wants to hire your dad," she said. "I don't think she likes him very much. I think he dogged on her the other night at the school board meeting."

Just then, Sarah put it together. Of course! Emerson's friend had the last name of Stein, and so did Max, the jerk from school who couldn't wait to put her in her place for no good reason. Still, she would have to have a campaign manager if she wanted to have any hope of getting the school board position. And it sounded like this Max Stein knew what he was doing. To say the least, if he worked in D.C. and managed real campaigns.

Julia shrugged her shoulders. "My dad can be a tool, but he's very good at what he does."

Sarah cocked her head. "So, he worked in D.C.? What inspired him to move here?"

"I don't know. He just got a wild hair one day and wanted to leave it all behind. Now he's working as an organic farmer."

"Huh," Sarah said. "Well, if he left it behind, he probably won't want to manage my campaign."

"Well, I'd still ask him. He works full-time as a farmer, but he takes people on as clients, too. He's managed a few small campaigns since he's been here."

A piece of the puzzle wasn't immediately obvious to Sarah. But she decided not to press it. "Sure, go ahead and give me his card and I'll give him a call," she said.

Emerson just gave Sarah a strange look. "Aunt Sarah, I think you should stand your ground. Don't kiss somebody's ass just because he can help you out."

Julia rolled her eyes. "Em's been on an anti-patriarchy kick since she broke up with Joe. Don't listen to her."

Sarah looked at Emerson, who was busy dragging a piece of her chicken through her mashed potatoes and gravy. "You broke up with Joe? Why didn't you say anything?"

"Nothing to say. He was all up in my business, thinking he owned me or something. I told him to butt out. And that was that."

Sarah furled her eyebrows. "Did you tell your mom?"

"No. It just happened. I'm sure you'll tell her though."

Sarah thought it was a shame because Joe seemed like such a good kid. At the same time, when she was Emerson's age, she went through boyfriends like she went through underwear. Emerson was definitely at that age when she was trying things out, asking herself where she fit in, who belonged in her life, and who didn't. And Emerson seemed more the independent type anyhow. She definitely didn't strike Sarah as the kind of girl who would allow anybody to try to tell her what to do. So, Joe might have overstepped her boundaries, and she wasn't going to put up with that for two seconds.

"Not my place. But I would encourage you to talk to Quinn about it."

"I will."

After dinner, Julia gave Sarah her father's phone number. "He doesn't really have any business cards for his campaign stuff. He doesn't do it enough to have business cards for it. But I know he manages people's races from time to time."

Sarah looked at the phone number and decided that she would call him.

Later.

Chapter Six

Ava

That Monday, Ava got some news that absolutely rocked her world.

Deacon was moving back to Australia.

"My sister's cancer is back," he said in distress. "And her husband has left her in the lurch. She's falling apart and afraid she'll die this time. She needs me."

Ava understood, of course. But it didn't mean her heart wasn't absolutely broken. She finally decided to give a man a chance, which was difficult for her because of what Christopher did. But she let her guard down and felt like she was absolutely falling in love with Deacon. And now it was all over.

"You have to go to your sister. She'll need you around for this battle and will need someone to help her out with the kids while she's taking chemo or immunotherapy or whatever treatment she's electing to try. It's just you and your sister left in your family, and you guys need to support each other."

Deacon's parents were killed in a boating accident when he was only 17, so he became a surrogate father to his sister. When his sister was diagnosed with non-Hodgkin's lymphoma, Deacon brought her to America to see a specialist at the Mayo Clinic in Minnesota. That was why he was brought to America in the first place. He met a woman, got married, divorced, and ended up on Nantucket Island.

Now, he was going back to Sydney, and there was nothing Ava could do about it. The whole thought made Ava want to vomit, but the last thing she would do was show her distress to Deacon. He didn't need any more stress in his life.

After Deacon dropped his bomb, Ava reacted the way she used to react when her heart broke – she sat on her deck, wrapped herself up in a blanket, and drank an entire bottle of wine. She thought about inviting over the ladies, but, at that moment, she just wanted to be alone. Alone with her thoughts, alone with her feelings. She just wasn't ready to verbalize all the things going through her head at that time.

After she finished one bottle of wine, she started on another. It was 11 o'clock by then and was extremely cold outside. Ava had the heat lamps going and a blanket, so she didn't really feel the cold March air. She was starting to feel a little sick because she wasn't used to drinking so much at once. Still, the physical part of her sickness at that time took her mind away from the emotional turmoil she was experiencing.

Was she in love with Deacon? She certainly was getting there. He was kind to her, fun, very interested in her life, an amazing piano player and general contractor, and she really enjoyed being around him. She'd overcome her misgivings about him and decided she would be all-in in the relationship. She had cautiously guarded her heart all this time, finally letting down her barriers, and it didn't work out. Again.

She was lost in thought when she heard a familiar voice behind her. It was Jessica. "Ava, I was looking for you. It's really cold out here, and you've been out all evening, so I'm just a little worried. Are you okay?"

Jessica was such a sweet girl. She was like Ava's surrogate daughter, a virtual fourth child. Jessica knew Ava had taken her in when she was at the lowest point in her life, and the young woman had managed to get it together since she started staying with Ava and working for her.

Ava just shook her head. "Actually, no. I'm very sad." Ava patted the chair seat next to her, and Jessica sat down. "How are you?" she slurred.

"Fine. I kinda miss Andrew, but otherwise, I'm fine."

Ava squinted at Jessica. "Oh, that's right. Andrew is in Los Angeles." He would be in Los Angeles for the next few weeks because he was working on a new recording. But he and Jessica had been in touch constantly. They'd known one another for under a year, but, it turned out, they went back a long way – they'd spent their early childhoods together. They were separated from one another when they were only five years old because of the tragedy that happened to Jessica's mother.

Jessica simply nodded her head but said nothing. "Now, you said you were sad. What's going on?"

Ava smiled wryly, took a sip of her wine and lightly

placed her hand on Jessica's shoulder. "Deacon is moving away to Australia. I'm 55 years old, and I've had my heart broken more than I can count. When my husband died all those years ago, I thought my heart had broken in two. It was the worst few years of my life after he died. Trying to raise three babies without a husband around, dealing with grief that almost broke me. And then I managed to fall in love again with Christopher. Against all odds. And he screwed me. And I kinda thought that that was the end. I wouldn't put myself out there again. I had my best friends, and then I had this bed-and-breakfast. I figured that was going to have to be enough for me."

"But you took a chance," Jessica said.

"Yes. I took a chance. And I lost. Big time. I don't blame him, not at all. His sister is in Australia, alone and scared, with two small children, a husband who has left, and a scary cancer diagnosis. She beat cancer before, making the recurrence much more serious. She needs him, and he has to go to her. But it doesn't make things any less sad for me."

Jessica just shook her head. "I'm so sorry. That has to be tough on both of you."

"More tough on him than me. He loves his sister very much." Ava shook her head and shivered just a little. "He's such a good man. He loves his sister like I love my children or my best friends. I would do anything for any of them. And if one of my children, or one of my friends, were in the same situation as Deacon's sister, alone and terrified, I would do the same for them as Deacon is doing for his sister. So, it's nobody's fault, and I greatly feel for him. In a way, I feel guilty. I'm sitting here being all depressed when he is the one who really needs to be depressed."

"Don't be silly. You also have a right to grieve. Don't deny yourself that, and don't try to minimize it. Speaking from experience, when you try to deny your tragedies, you really get into trouble."

Ava just nodded her head. "I'm feeling it even more than I should because I don't have much going on in my life right now. My business has been very slow, and you've been doing everything around the inn, so I have a lot of time to sit around and stew in my juices."

Since Jessica was staying there at the inn for free, and she was drawing a decent salary from Ava, she was working full time. And, considering that the place was only 25% full on any given day, Jessica did everything that needed to be done around the bed and breakfast. She insisted on that, and Ava, knowing that Jessica had her pride and wanted to work for her free room and board and salary, didn't mind Jessica doing all the work.

The upshot was that Ava didn't have much to do at all and wasn't doing well with her downtime. She was used to hard work, putting in long hours. When the children were young, she worked full-time at the law firm while bringing up three children on her own, with the help of Hallie, who was a lifesaver because she watched her triplets while she worked.

Even after the kids had grown and found their own lives – Jackson was an actor in Los Angeles, Samantha was working at a bakery in Brooklyn while living with Grayson, her roommate who now was her boyfriend, and Charlotte was married with a small child – Ava still was extremely busy because she was working at the law firm some 80 hours a week. And then she arrived in Nantucket and had been super busy with her bed-and-breakfast.

Samantha was now living on the island and was a highly sought-after wedding cake designer. She was head over heels for Grayson, the roommate who had been in love with her for years but never thought she'd feel the same way. Samantha eventually came around to Grayson's affections, and the two couldn't be more well-matched.

During the summer months, Ava had a lot going on around the business. So, she was used to not having a lot of downtime. Now she had nothing but downtime and wasn't doing well with it.

And now, this. Deacon moving to Australia was throwing her for a complete loop because she didn't have work to take her mind off her sorrow.

Jessica took Ava's hand, and this comforting gesture told Ava all she needed to know about her surrogate daughter. Jessica was there for her.

"Can I ask you a question?" Jessica said after the two had sat in the silence and listened to the waves roll in. "I don't want to pry."

"Sure. Ask away. I've got nothing to hide."

"The guy who was here the other day – was that Christopher? Your former husband?"

Ava cocked her head. "Yes." Then she suddenly remembered the look of recognition that Jessica had given Christopher, and Christopher had given back to Jessica. "You know him, don't you?"

Jessica just shrugged her shoulders. "I do. But I can't tell you how I know him."

Ava understood. Jessica didn't say as much, but Ava felt that Jessica might have seen him at one of her AA meetings. Ava knew that one of the rules that people who go to five-step meetings follow is not to divulge any information about anybody at the meetings with them.

She also knew that people who attend AA meetings aren't necessarily alcoholics but might be struggling with another kind of addiction. But they go to the AA meetings because, in the end, addiction is addiction, and it's not always easy to find meetings for other kinds of addiction such as drugs or gambling. That was Jessica's issue – she had confided in Ava that she never had a problem with alcohol, just prescription painkillers, but she couldn't find a meeting that was specific for narcotics, so she went to the AA meetings instead.

"Say no more."

"I won't. But, you told me what he did to you. And trust me, that was really an epic betrayal. But I wanted you to understand the nature of addiction."

Jessica paused and watched the waves some more. She still had Ava's hand, and her eyes had a faraway look. Ava silently waited for her to go on.

Jessica took a deep breath. "When you're chasing the Dragon, whatever that Dragon happens to be, that's all you can think about. And you'll do anything, absolutely anything, for your personal Dragon. You'll lie, cheat, and steal. You don't care about other people when you're addicted, so you'll step on everyone you used to love. You only care about your Dragon. That was the reason why my parents kicked me out. I was desperate to keep using, so I stole from them all the time and didn't care that I stole from them. I lied to them, right to their faces. I was a very different person when I was desperate to get my OxyContin, and that was literally my only focus in life."

Ava knew where Jessica was going. And Jessica had a point. Jessica still wasn't speaking with her parents, even though she'd kicked her addiction and was in therapy. She'd turned her life around, but her parents apparently couldn't forget how she acted when she lived under their roof, so they still were not taking her phone calls or answering her emails. Ava thought that was terrible of them – if one of her children had problems with addiction, she wouldn't cut them off, even if they did steal from her and lie to her. And, if her addicted child turned his or her life around, she really would be there to support them.

Yet, Jessica's parents had turned their backs on her, and they continued to do so even though Jessica had completely kicked her addiction and was really good. Ava even tried to call Jessica's parents, but they wouldn't speak with her.

"I know what you're saying. Christopher had an addiction, and he was desperate, which led him to do what he did. And I suppose in your mind, he really can't be blamed for what he did. It wasn't him who took all that money. It was his gambling addiction."

Jessica nodded her head. "It's a disease, addiction. It takes hold of you and becomes your obsession in life. And one thing I've been doing as part of my therapy is learning about what causes addictions. It's hereditary, it's neurological, it's brain pathways, it's chemical, it's physical. It's often an outlet for depression or mental illness. Or, for me, PTSD. It was my balm. Since learning about it, I've been slowly working towards forgiving myself for my behavior. I've been starting to understand that I've not been entirely to blame for getting addicted to OxyContin."

"Well, you had a horrible trauma when you were very young. You didn't process it because you blocked it out. So it's understandable that you would turn to substances to help you cope with life. Christopher doesn't necessarily have the same story as you did. In fact, he had a decent life, one that he threw away when he left me without a word after stealing over $1 million from me."

Jessica grimaced. "I wouldn't be so sure that Christopher had such a great life before he turned to gambling."

"You know something, don't you?" Ava asked her. "You

know something I probably don't about why Christopher turned to gambling and threw everything away."

Jessica nodded her head. "I do. But, of course, I can't say anything to you about him. About what I know about him. Confidentiality. But I just wanted to hint that there's a lot he hasn't told you. Not that anything he might tell you about what happened will change your mind about him. It probably won't. He betrayed you, took away your safe zone, and I don't necessarily blame you if you never wanted to speak to him again. But, at the same time, I would love it if you would keep an open mind about him."

Ava faced the surf, which was pounding in her ears. She had consumed a bottle and 1/2 of wine and was starting to feel nauseated. Like she was seasick, the icky twisty feeling that your feet were not rooted on the ground.

What Jessica was telling Ava was something she'd known all along. Christopher was sick when he stole from her and left her. He was sick, just like her friend Hallie was sick with cancer. Hallie was on the mend from her cancer and was almost done with chemo. According to the last scan, she was cancer-free.

Addiction was a bit different from having cancer, but it was all the same in certain ways. Just like a person can't necessarily prevent getting cancer, or meningitis, which afflicted her daughter Charlotte's baby girl, you certainly couldn't always avoid getting addicted. Many people believed that people who couldn't quit drinking, smoking, doing drugs, overeating, or gambling had some kind of a moral failing. That they chose to self-destruct. But Ava knew in her heart that that wasn't right. Nobody would choose self-destruction if they had a true say in the matter.

It was a bit like mental illness, really. She had known many people over her life who suffered from depression or bipolar or OCD or PTSD, or any number of mental problems. And all of them said they would rather have a physical disease than a mental one. People weren't necessarily blamed for having diabetes, say, and people suffering from physical illnesses attracted sympathy. But the people who suffer from mental illness were blamed. Stigmatized. Told by people who had normal brains that they needed just to get over it. But it wasn't as easy as that. You couldn't just get over a chemical imbalance in the brain, which was often the cause of depression, bipolar, schizophrenia, or any number of mental illnesses.

And she knew that addiction was much like that – you couldn't necessarily just get over your addiction without some kind of intervention or hitting rock bottom. She wondered if Christopher had hit rock bottom. Perhaps he did, and maybe that was the catalyst for him to change.

She knew the right answer. She knew she should talk to Christopher. She should find out what happened to him over the past couple of years and why he got addicted in the first place. Not that she would ever take him back. She didn't know that that was even on the table, anyhow. But even if it were, she still didn't think she would ever trust him again.

But she should at least hear him out. Especially since he was going to be on the same island as her. There was no point in trying to ignore him if she ran into him. They were two mature adults, so there was no reason that they couldn't speak as two adults would speak.

"Do you happen to know where he's living?" Ava asked Jessica. "Forget that. Do you happen to know why he's here?"

Jessica nodded her head. "Yes, and yes. If you want, if I

see him again, I can ask him to call you or for his phone number."

Ava shook her head. "Nah. On second thought, that wouldn't be such a good idea. I don't think I'm ready to face this particular issue. I'm reeling from the Deacon thing, and I don't know if I have the bandwidth to deal with anything else right now. But, even if I don't necessarily want him to call me right now, I might want his phone number."

That seemed like a reasonable thing. *Don't call me, I'll call you. Or maybe not.* She wanted the ball in her court. She didn't want to be put on the spot by having Christopher call her. But, if she ever came around on speaking to him, she wanted the option of calling him and meeting him on her terms.

Jessica nodded her head. "I think that that would be a good idea. I don't know if I'll be seeing him, but I'll get his number for you if I do."

"Okay."

Ava looked at her watch. She saw it was past midnight. And she realized, all at once, that she was very tired.

"Well, I'm glad you came out to talk to me. I thought I wanted to be alone, so I didn't call Sarah and them. But I think you've helped me focus on something that's been nagging me. It's been a battle between hating him and feeling sorry for him. I hate him for what he did. But there's always been a part of me that has felt real empathy for him. I've never had to deal with mental illness or addiction in my own life. I've been very lucky that way, and I know it. So it's difficult for me to see somebody else's issue and separate it from their actions. But you've reminded me there's always another side of the story."

Jessica smiled. "There always is. I know it's a cliché, but it always helps to walk in another person's shoes. You gave me a chance. You didn't need to. When I came to you, I'd only been sober for a short period of time. For all you knew, I would've stolen the silverware from you to pay for my next hit. But you took a chance on me, and I'll be forever grateful for that. And I feel like the chance you gave me is something I should pay forward. I'm helping other people who are struggling with addictions. And one of those things I do is try to help other people understand what we go through."

Ava smiled and put her arm around Jessica. "Food for thought. Anyhow, it's time to hit the hay. I'll see you in the morning."

Ava went to her bed and tried not to cry herself to sleep.

Chapter Seven

Sarah

Sarah nervously went to Max Stein's farm. She was going to go and buy a flat of pastured eggs and any kind of produce she could get from the place. And she would hopefully talk to Max and ask him if he minded taking over her school campaign.

She drove up, observing the cows and chickens grazing in a field. She was happy to buy the eggs from this place because the chickens apparently were treated quite well. That was always important to Sarah because she was big on animal welfare and usually was a proponent of knowing the source of her food. She wasn't always able to trace her meat and produce to a family farm – she shopped at the supermarket like everybody else – but her preference was to buy local and speak with farmers about how they raised their animals and grew their produce.

She was dressed in jeans, a tank top, and a jean jacket. It

was an unseasonably warm day for March on Nantucket, and she felt somewhat relaxed by the weather.

She approached a white building that housed the eggs and produce and walked in the door. The wooden floors creaked beneath her feet, and the building was fairly spacious, with a high ceiling marked by exposed wooden beams. Behind the counter was a young woman who was around 25 years old. Her long blonde hair was tied back in a low ponytail, and she had a friendly smile.

"I'm Gretchen. Can I help you?" she asked Sarah.

Sarah nodded her head. "I'd like a flat of 30 pastured eggs." She also noticed some flat tables on the side of the road that led up to the farm, underneath an awning. On the tables were various fruits and vegetables – lettuce, carrots, radishes, onions, garlic, and avocados. The avocados obviously were brought in from another part of the country, as they did not grow native there on Nantucket.

The young lady gave Sarah the flat of eggs and rang them up. "Is there anything else I can do for you?" she asked.

Sarah nodded her head. "Yes. I'd like to know how I can talk to Mr. Stein. I know he owns this farm, and I always like to talk to the farmer to see what their practices are. Is there any way I can talk to him?"

"Well, he works from six in the morning to 3 o'clock in the afternoon," Gretchen said. "And he hosts a farm tour every Saturday morning at 9. He goes through the history of his farm, talks about sustainability issues, gives lectures on organic gardening and renewable energy and how he uses wind turbines and solar panels to power his farm. The tour is free. You should attend."

"The history of his farm? I wasn't aware he'd been on

the island long. I hear that he was living in D.C. before he moved here."

"Well, this farm has been in his family for generations. He inherited it when his father passed away. For about 10 years, though, it was run by other people he'd hired. He took it over to farm it himself two years ago."

"Just curious," Sarah said. "This seems like such a change in scenery from somebody who had come from the fast-paced world of D.C. politics. Do you know what brought him here?"

Gretchen had a look that told Sarah she probably had no idea why Max would've left his high-powered D.C. job to come to sleepy Nantucket and take over a farm. She shrugged her shoulders. "I think he just wanted something lower key than what he was experiencing in D.C. I don't know. I never really asked him that question."

Sarah just nodded her head. "Well, thanks for the eggs. I'll stop by the little stand on my way out and pick up some produce. And I think I'll take you up on taking the farm tour on Saturday morning. That might be interesting. I've always wanted to learn more about organic gardening, and I think taking a tour would be very enlightening."

"Hope to see you Saturday morning!" Gretchen said brightly.

Sarah put the eggs in her car, then walked down to the stand and bought some lettuce, cabbage, carrots, and radishes. And then, she drove home and put the farm tour for Saturday morning on her calendar.

Sarah drove to Max's farm that Saturday morning to attend his lecture and farm tour. She took a seat with about 10 other women and men and listened to Max talk about his farming methods, lecture on the importance of using renewable energy in farming, how to amend the soil to get the best crops, and about the history of his farm.

He kept looking at her as if he was trying to place her face. At some point, it was obvious that he remembered exactly who she was – he had a look on his face of recognition. However, he didn't smile or look slightly friendly towards her.

After the talk, Max walked through his farm, and the small crowd trailed behind. "Meet my hens," he said, pointing to the 20 or so chickens bobbing their heads around the field, pecking at the grass and caw-cawing at one another. "They're never in a cage, although they have a shelter where they build their nests, and they're free to come and go. I have names for all of them, and I call them my girls. And I have one rooster because it's important for the pecking order. He can protect the hens from predators, breaks up fights between the hens, and struts around like he owns the place. His name is Fabio."

Everybody started to giggle a little bit about the rooster named Fabio.

A little girl raised her hand. Max looked at her and smiled, and then pointed to her.

"What are the hens' names?" she asked politely. She was a pretty little girl with blonde hair and blue eyes, and she was there with her mother, who looked like an older version of the little girl. The girl looked like she could be Sarah's child, and Sarah got a little pang in her heart. She could imagine, in another life, bringing her child to this. It was just the kind of thing a little kid would like, touring a farm and seeing the animals.

Max smiled. "Amelia Egghart, Princess Layanegg,

Meryl Cheep, Julia Eggberts, Hennifer Aniston, Hennifer Lopez, Hennifer Lawrence, Hennifer Garner, Charlays Theron, Scarlett Johenson, Ann Henaway, Goldie Hen, Hen Solo, Gwyneth Poultry, Yolko Ono, Henny From Heaven, Henny For Your Thoughts, Henny Marshall and Henna Bonham Carter," he said with a smile. "Also, Elsa and Anna. My daughter was a big *Frozen* fan, so I named those two to honor her."

His face briefly darkened when he mentioned his daughter, and Sarah wondered why.

The little girl giggled, and her eyes got big. "Which ones are Elsa and Anna?" she asked, obviously a *Frozen* fan.

Max pointed to two of the hens, a fat yellow one and an even fatter red one. "Elsa," he said, pointing to the yellow one. "And Anna," he said, pointing to the red one.

The little girl bent down and tried to pet Anna, but the hen wasn't having it, and she ran away.

"I see you're an Anna fan," Max said with a smile.

The little girl said nothing but just nodded her head.

The group walked along further, and they happened upon a small pen of goats and sheep. "This is the petting farm," Max said and smiled at the little girl. "And something tells me you're going to make good friends with these baaaaaad little sheep and goats."

The little girl eagerly nodded her head, and she led her mother into the petting zoo. Other tour members, including Sarah, also went into the pen to pet the animals. She might've been 53 years old, but she was a small child when it came to petting zoos. She loved them.

Max gave everybody a handful of feed. Sarah went into the pen with the little girl and a few adults and eagerly pet the sheep, goats, and the occasional alpaca.

Max was talking with one of the women, who was

asking him if the goats and sheep also had names. He said they did, and they had names like Leonardo DiCaprigoat, Selena Goatmez, Ryan Goatling, Emma Goat, Vincent Van Goat, and the Great Goatsby. The sheep had names like Baaad Mama Jama, Baaabara Streisand, Baaarack Obama and Albert Ramstein.

The alpaca was apparently named Doe Eyes. "Because that's what she looks like with those big beautiful brown eyes," Max said. "A doe."

Sarah smiled in spite of herself. Max seemed to have a good sense of humor, judging by what he named his animals.

After Sarah petted the animals and fed them the special feed Max supplied, she and everybody left the petting zoo and followed Max through the rest of the farm. He grew lettuce, cabbage, leeks, radishes, Swiss chard, winter wheat and Brussels sprouts.

"These are my winter crops," he explained. "These are the best plants to grow when cold like this. When spring gets here, I'll be growing tomatoes, green beans, squash, peppers, broccoli, cucumbers, summer wheat, barley and lots and lots of corn."

One of the women walked along with him. "I have an awful time trying to grow my own garden," she said to him. She noticed a head of cabbage the size of a bowling ball. "How do you get such lush and beautiful vegetables?"

"Farming is both an art and a science. You must understand what nutrients your soil needs and the right amount of potassium, nitrogen and phosphorous. You have to get just the right blend of nutrients. Otherwise, your crops won't thrive. I devote my entire life to this, studying my crops, identifying any problems I might have with them, and studying all the remedies of issues that might arise."

She nodded. "Do you have any specific recommendations?"

"Bring over some of your soil, and I can analyze it and let you know what you need and how to add it. That's one of the services I provide."

After about an hour of walking and talking through the farm and listening to Max talk about how several generations of his family had tended to the land, they finally arrived at a small restaurant towards the farm entrance.

"Feel free to grab a bite in my little restaurant. I also have several kinds of craft beer I brew on site. I make the beer with the wheat and barley I grow on this land. All the food is fresh, farm to table, which is important because most produce loses nutrients within 24 hours of harvesting. That's why it's important to buy locally and support Nantucket farmers. At my restaurant, the veggies are completely fresh. I don't actually slaughter my own animals – the animals on my farm are strictly here for breeding or as pets, as with the sheep, goats, and alpaca in the petting zoo. But I get my meat from other local farms, and it's also very fresh."

Sarah and the group walked into the restaurant, and Sarah ordered a craft beer. She took a table by a window, and, before her food arrived, Max approached her table.

"I think I remember you," he said to her. "School board meeting?"

"Yes. That was me."

He smiled. "Oh, yes. You're the social justice warrior who seems to haunt my nightmares. Attend any rallies for trans bathrooms lately?"

Sarah didn't know whether she should feel offended or amused. She supposed it was his way of making a joke, so she smiled. "Well, as it happens, I was going to organize a riot with my suburban friends. We were going to burn our bras in the street and fly rainbow flags everywhere."

"Count me out," he said with a smile. "Did you enjoy the tour?"

"Of course. I try to tour farms as much as possible, as I always like to know where my food comes from. And you're very knowledgeable. That was part of the reason why I wanted to come on this tour. I also wanted to come to the tour to talk to you about something else."

He sat down. "Intriguing. I'm all corn ears."

"Right. Well, your daughter, Julia, stayed at my house the other night. She's friends with my friend's daughter, Emerson. And she told me that you used to manage political campaigns in D.C. and occasionally take clients here on Nantucket. And I was thinking –"

He raised an eyebrow and smirked. "Let me just stop you. Yes, if I believe in their positions, I take on occasional clients for local races. Somehow I think you're going to ask me to manage a campaign for you because you're running for school board, and if that's the case, the answer is no."

Sarah cocked her head. She wasn't used to being turned down flat. Especially not by men. "Aren't you even going to listen to my pitch?" she asked him.

"Nope. I know everything I need to know about you and your views on school-related issues, and I have no interest in furthering the leftist agenda in school."

Sarah felt her hackles rising again. "Really? Are you so closed-minded?" Then she grimaced. "Don't tell me you're one of those guys who see critical race theory in every textbook."

He cocked his head. "Now, who's being closed-minded? No, I'm not one of the people who see critical race theory in every textbook. I think our children should learn about racial justice and slavery. I don't think our nation's history should be whitewashed. But I can't get on board with your position on book banning. Sorry. I think there are books our students shouldn't be exposed to, and that's that."

"I'm surprised you don't have an ostrich around because you sure do like creatures who bury their head in the sand," Sarah said.

Max rolled his eyes. "Very funny. You should have a job on my farm. I'm in the market for a stand-up comedian to bring the folks into the restaurant. I'd hire you in a second."

Sarah shook her head. "So you think our children should just have their minds protected from scary concepts, do you? Don't you think that learning about controversial subjects opens their minds and teaches them about critical thinking, tolerance, and different worldviews? They'll be exposed to a cruel world when they leave the nest, and it's best to prepare them."

His face clouded over, and Sarah saw the same expression she briefly saw when he talked about his daughter who loved *Frozen*.

"The answer is no. Listen, I'm on one of the advisory panels on which books should be taken out of the library. I definitely am not on board with keeping certain titles that many of the parents are in favor of keeping. So why would I help a woman get elected who wants to go against my work? I have an uphill battle and don't need any more opposition on the board."

Sarah narrowed her eyes. "I think that's just an excuse. I think you don't want to help me because I don't have a kid in the school, so I don't have a say."

He shook his head. "Why do you care so much about what books are in the school's library? It's not like you're going to have the worry about a kid coming home to you after having read a book featuring murder and rape, asking you questions about it, and having nightmares. And you don't know what might happen if the wrong book gets into the wrong hands."

"I care about what books are available in the school's library because I often babysit my friend's kid, Emerson. She's a very bright child and reads a lot, and I want her to have access to every controversial book she can get her hands on. She's thoughtful, wants to learn about the world, and wants to hear different viewpoints. And I want that for her."

"Then take her to the public library. You can get any books you want there. No need to pollute the middle school library with trash that'll destroy young minds."

Sarah crossed her arms in front of her. "So, you won't take me on as a client?"

Max's face seemed to soften. "Listen, my full-time job is my farm. Period. Full stop. So, I try to limit my campaign management business to maybe one or two clients a year. If that. I really enjoy what I'm doing now. It's so much more low-stress than what I was doing. So, saying that I'm extremely particular about who I take on would be an understatement. Don't take it personally. But I must be excited about somebody before I can take them on. I think you'd agree that's a good idea. And I certainly am not going to take on somebody who will be an opponent on the school board, which you will be. So, the answer is no."

Sarah bit her bottom lip. "Okay. I guess there's no changing your mind."

"No. Now, what can I interest you in here at the restaurant? I have some fantastic craft beers, and our salads are second to none. You look like a girl who likes a good salad."

Sarah did like a good salad, but she didn't feel like

eating right at that moment. "I'm good," she said. "I'll be sure to pick up some more produce on my way out, though."

He shrugged his shoulders. "Suit yourself."

Then he got up, went behind the bar, and started pouring for a group of people who had just entered the restaurant.

Sarah quietly left without saying goodbye.

Chapter Eight

Ava

For about a week after Ava had her talk with Jessica and said goodbye to Deacon for the last time, it seemed Ava couldn't go anywhere without running into Christopher. She went to the farmer's market, and there he was, talking to some vendors about CBD. She went to A Brotherhood of Thieves, a popular bar in the basement of a building built in the 1840s. It was one of her favorite places to go to unwind, open year round.

There he was, sitting in front of the fireplace, nursing a beer. As he was at the farmers market, he was alone in the bar.

Both times, Ava's instinct was to walk the other way, in the case of the farmers market, and, in the case of the bar, she had the instinct just to leave. She was there with Hallie, Quinn and Sarah, and when she turned to them and said she wanted to try another place, the ladies groaned.

"Ava, sugar, this guy seems to have some kind of radar

for where you're going to be," Quinn said. "You'll have to go over and talk to him or ignore him. What you can't do is avoid him. Aren't you curious about why he's here in the first place? I sure am."

Ava shook her head. "No. I'm not curious about why he's hanging around this island. I just wish he would go away."

"You can wish all you want, but he's with you here on this tiny island. Now, I know he ruined your life. And I know that we were plotting his demise when he ruined your life. I wanted to boil him in oil. You wanted something faster and cleaner, and less painful. I think you said you wanted him to have a carbon monoxide leak in his house and die peacefully in his sleep."

Quinn was referring to the night when Ava, Hallie and Quinn were sitting on Ava's rooftop terrace in New York City, fantasizing about Christopher's death. They had just seen the movie *9-5,* as it had come on TCM, and they were talking about the three ladies in that movie plotting the death of their boss. The ladies started doing the same thing about Christopher, talking about their revenge fantasies for him.

In the end, Ava wimped out in a way. She didn't want him to die a painful death. But she wanted him off the face of the earth, so she said that maybe his house should just spring a carbon monoxide leak, and he could just go to sleep and not wake up again.

Hallie smiled at Ava. She was out with the ladies, which was a good sign because she had been battling cancer and hadn't felt like getting out of the house lately. But she was feeling better, and this cheered Ava immensely. "Ava, I'm with Quinn. It couldn't hurt to just go over there and talk to him. I know we hated that guy for all this time. But maybe it's time to make nice."

Ava grimaced, took another sip of beer, and then walked over to where Christopher was sitting in front of the fireplace. She resisted the urge to bark at him and tell him that he wasn't welcome in this bar, on this island, on this earth. She tried to remember the words Jessica told her about addiction. How it wasn't really his fault. How he was sick. How she should have empathy for him.

She took a deep breath as she stood in front of him. He didn't notice she was there at first. He was too busy staring into his beer with a baleful expression. She finally cleared her throat, and he looked up.

He looked startled, his brown eyes getting wide, and he jumped just a little when she made a noise. "Ava, I'm so sorry. I wasn't expecting you. I thought it was going to be the waitress."

She swallowed hard. "No, it's me."

He nodded his head. "Okay. Well, you're welcome to join me. As you can see, I'm alone."

Ava sat down. "So, how are you?"

"How does it look like I am?" Christopher's words were slurring just a bit. "I'm sitting here in a bar, completely alone. And that seems to be the story of my life lately. I've been completely alone for some time. For years, really. Even during the final years of my marriage with you, I've been completely alone."

"Oh, spare me," Ava blurted out. He was about to rehash the lament he always told the marriage counselors they had been seeing for the last five years of their union. He always complained she was never around, and she would tell the counselor the same thing about him. He wasn't exactly a guy who was there for her. He had long since emotionally checked out of the relationship years before physically leaving for good.

"Ava, believe it or not, I wish I could spare you. I don't want to be on this island any more than you want me here. But I'm stuck here for the time being." He looked sadly into his beer. "Don't get me wrong, I was going to seek you out at some point. But fate has brought me here now. Fate, and destiny."

Ava took a deep breath. "Christopher, you're not making any sense. And I don't understand a lot of things. I don't know why you're here. I don't know how you got the money to pay me back. And I don't know why you can't leave."

"Ava, it's a long story. You're asking me all these questions, but I know what you want to ask me. Why did I self-destruct? I had everything. At least, for a while, I had everything. A job where I was making a half-million dollars a year. A lovely wife. We had something good at one time, but then something happened. We just drifted. And then I started to self-destruct. Why don't you start there? Why don't you start asking questions about that?"

Ava knew she should start there, but she didn't want to. It was too painful to rehash the breakdown of their marriage. It was a chicken or egg thing – did the breakdown of their marriage lead to the gambling, or did the gambling, and the fact that he was shutting her out of the fact that he was battling addiction, accelerate the breakdown of the marriage?

"Christopher, I don't know what you want from me. I've moved on. I have a good life now. I have a thriving business, live on a beautiful island, my best friends are around me, and my sister is back in my life. I'm even on good terms with my mother. I don't know why I'm being forced to deal with a toxic part of my existence. And that's what you are – you're toxic to me."

Christopher visibly flinched. "Wow. I didn't know that I was some kind of poison in your life."

"Well, you were. The saddest thing was that after you left, I didn't grieve. I was angry, but only because you stole all that money. But I didn't look to your side of the bed and feel a hole in my heart. I didn't walk around the city streets, sadly going to restaurants we went to, galleries we used to haunt in our early days, the opera and the theater and mournfully think of you."

As Ava spoke, the memories did start to flood back to her. There were happy times between them. Of course there were. They got married, after all. There was love - things in common, laughter, staying up until 2 o'clock in the morning talking. They had season tickets to the symphony and to the Met. They both enjoyed the works of Puccini and tried to see every opera written by the legendary composer and librettist. Christopher was much more knowledgeable about what was happening in these operas because he had studied Puccini as an undergrad at NYU. His passion for *La Bohème*, *Tosca*, *Madame Butterfly* and *Turandot* was Ava's introduction to the world of opera, leading her to seek out other famous composers and other genres of opera.

He expanded her horizons. He wasn't just into the opera, but he was into art exhibits at the Metropolitan Museum of Art. They went to see a different one every Saturday they were free. They went to Broadway shows, frequented many five-star restaurants and holes in the wall, and just devoured the city together.

At least five years before he left, all that ceased. It wasn't just that they were both working all the time, although that was part of it. But Ava knew that wasn't the only break-down, because they were always busy with their jobs, even when they first met and were falling in love. It was just that, early on in the relationship, they made time for each other. Even if they each worked 60 to 70 hours a week, they ensured they had at least one date night a week and slept in the same bed every night.

And then it changed. It was gradual, and then all at once. At first, it was just that Christopher stopped calling her during the day. He used to call her from his job to chat for five or 10 minutes during a break in the action. Just to tell her he was thinking about her. But those phone calls started becoming less and less.

And then the date nights completely disappeared. Saturday nights, their standing night to go out on the town, became nights Christopher chose to spend with friends instead of her. Or, they made excuses about why they didn't want to go out. Ava found herself going to the opera, the theater and the Met museum with Hallie and/or Quinn instead of Christopher.

They got out of sync at some point and could never quite get back into sync. Ava still didn't know exactly why it happened, let alone when it happened. She only knew it happened.

So, by the time he finally left, there was nothing left to grieve. And maybe it was that she had already done all the grieving. She already had her opera and theater buddy, and it wasn't him anymore. It was either Quinn or Hallie, some-times both. She went to gallery exhibits with them, not him. So it was more of a gentle transition than a jarring change in her life.

And the fact that he took all their money sealed his betrayal. That was what made her vomit, not the fact that he was gone. And then she felt sad that the stolen money was the only reason she was sad.

Now, here he was. And Ava wasn't feeling the feelings that she probably should've been. There was no longing, no looking into his eyes and thinking about what should have been. No regrets about the way things ended. There was just nothingness.

Yet, a part of her did have a certain amount of pity for him. There was a scrap that she could build on and maybe at least allow herself to forgive him for doing what he did. There was a part of her that was open to hearing his story.

What there wasn't was a part of her that would ever allow him back into her life romantically.

Ava cocked her head. "Okay. I must admit that my curiosity is getting the best of me here. And you do look pretty pathetic, just sitting here nursing a beer, all by yourself in this bar. So, if you'd like to have dinner, I'll be open to that. If only to shut the door, get some closure. Maybe see things through your eyes."

His face seemed to brighten when she said that. "Ava, I'd really like that. You've always been so much better than me. I'm just warning you, when I tell you the story of my self-destruction and why I hit rock bottom, you might just hate me more. But that's a chance I'm willing to take."

"I'm intrigued. Because I really don't hate you. I see you as a lost soul, but I don't hate you. So, you're telling me you're going to tell me a story that'll cause me to hate you. Is that what you're saying?"

He nodded his head. "That's what I'm saying. But I've been doing a 12-step program for the past two years, and I've come to the point in my program where I have to make amends with the people I've hurt. I can't move on until I do that. So, I think I really need to make amends to you. And that means I have to come clean to you about what drove me to the gambling table. You're going to hate me."

Ava sighed. "Christopher, I have no big emotions for you anymore. I don't think I have the bandwidth to have any feelings for you anymore. So, whatever you say to me, I don't see myself becoming particularly enraged. So, don't worry about whatever you have to say to me. I can handle it."

Christopher and Ava made a date to have dinner the following evening at The Straight Wharf. It was Christopher's idea to go there. He had been on the island for only a week, but he apparently was already aware of the best places to eat in town.

Ava returned to the table where Quinn, Hallie and Sarah were waiting for her. "Well, I did it. I ripped the Band-Aid off. I made a date to hang out with him tomorrow night at the Straight Wharf."

Sarah, who was next to Ava, put her hand on her sister's arm. "I never knew the guy, but Hallie and Quinn have been filling me in on what went down between the two of you. That guy seems like a real jerk."

"He was. But only because he stole money. Not because he left, necessarily. And I have a feeling that something even worse was going on behind the scenes I wasn't aware of. At any rate, I don't hate him, and because I don't, there's nothing he can tell me that will devastate my heart. So, don't worry about me. I'm mainly going out to dinner with him because, well, I'm damn curious."

Sarah had tears in her eyes. "Sis, I'm worried about you. I know the Deacon thing is bothering you more than you let on. I just don't want you to go down a rabbit hole where you get sucked into something you shouldn't be because you're reeling."

Sarah, unfortunately, knew Ava better than Ava sometimes knew herself. That's what sisters were for, to remind you exactly who you are. Even when you sometimes want to deny your basic nature, your sibling knows what's in your heart.

"I love you, Sarah, but this is not a case of Jake McCallister dumping me, which threw me into the arms of Ryan Hamilton." Ava was referring to one of her short-lived high school romances that went sour when Jake McAllister, the guy Ava was crushing on, dumped her for another girl. This led Ava into the unfortunate arms of Ryan Hamilton, a boy who had many problems at home and ended up hitting her when she accidentally pushed over his motorcycle.

But Sarah was right about one thing – Ava was still reeling from the Deacon thing. She told the ladies that it was all well and good. She didn't know him all that well, and she always thought in her heart that it wasn't going to go over in the end. She felt almost silly for being as depressed as she was about it.

But she *did* know him well. They had lots of great talks, walks along the beach, and evenings in front of the fireplace in her room. He was a gentle, generous lover, and he really stimulated her physical self and her mental self. She didn't think that she really belonged with him. He was too handsome, too young, too much. Yet, for whatever reason, he did seem to really like her and made her feel special while he was around.

And now he was gone. And she was going to have to reassure the ladies that she was not getting sucked back into Christopher's web. "Sarah, I just wanted you to know that there is zero chance I'll get involved romantically with the man. But I do need to make nice with him. So, I'm going to hear him out."

"Whatever you do, we'll support you," Hallie reassured her. "You've always made the right decision. And you'll make the right decision here, too. So, don't worry."

Ava took a deep breath. "Okay. Now, enough about me. Sarah, what's happening with you and your school board thing?"

Sarah shrugged her shoulders. "I tried to interest Max Stein in taking over my campaign, but he wants nothing to do with me. He tells me he doesn't like my agenda even though he doesn't really know what the agenda is. So, unless I can figure out another campaign manager, I'll have to run for school board on my own. And I have to tell you, I don't know the first thing about what to do. I guess I need to fundraise and all that and get volunteers. Maybe find a storefront for my campaign, although I think that would be silly and an added expense I don't really need. I can probably just run it from home. But I really wish I had a professional to help me. I'm a total novice and don't know what I'm doing."

Quinn took a sip of her wine and smiled at Sarah. "I think it's fantastic you're getting involved. I wish I had the time. Every time Emerson comes home and tells me what's going on in her school, I wish I could just go in there and help change the culture of the place. I don't know how these reactionaries got on that school board, but I do know they need to be stopped."

Sarah's back got a little straighter. "I agree, even if I don't have a kid in that school." And then she looked at Hallie. "Hey, maybe I can hire you to help me with the campaign. After all, you're doing the life coach thing. Maybe you can coach me, help me get the confidence to do this sort of thing."

Hallie smiled. "Sarah, I certainly can help you gain

confidence in yourself. That's part of what I do. I can help you drill down on your strengths and weaknesses and how you can use them to your advantage. But, with all due respect, I don't know anything about campaigns either. But I know many people who run for school board don't have a manager. Maybe I can help you find other people you can get in touch with who might be able to help you. You know, other school board members."

"Well, I guess we can start with the confidence thing. And I'd love it if you could work with me to find people who might be able to help me."

"I'll help with that too," Quinn said eagerly. "After all, sugar, I know a lot of rich folks around this island now. I've got the contacts to help you. And, who knows? Maybe I can wrangle one of those guys to host a fundraiser for you."

Ava eagerly nodded her head too. "I can get Samantha to make a cake for your fundraiser. It'll be fun!"

Sarah just smiled. "Let's not get too ahead of ourselves. I've got to figure out the basics of running before I can ask people for money. And I need to flesh out my positions, not just on the book banning thing, but on other issues facing the school. Although I'll use the book banning thing as a springboard and a focus for the campaign. But, ladies, I love your enthusiasm. Let me do the research, and then, Quinn, maybe you can put me in touch with somebody who might be able to host a fundraiser or introduce me to a campaign manager. And then Ava can talk to Samantha about making a cake. For now, I just want Hallie to brainstorm with me."

The ladies all clinked their glasses.

Tomorrow evening Ava was going to hopefully get some answers from Christopher. She felt stressed just thinking about having to sit down with him for a meal. But, for now, she would have fun with her friends.

Chapter Nine

Sarah

Sarah and Hallie met the following evening. Hallie was going to help Sarah brainstorm her strengths and weaknesses, her interests and any psychological blocks she might have. Sarah thought this was a good way to start. She wanted to get to the bottom of her motivations and how that would translate to the average voter.

Sarah also wanted Hallie to help her get organized. There were forms to fill out, funds to raise, and a petition that needed to be circulated. She had no clue about how to do any of that, and she wanted someone to help her, even if it was like the blind leading the blind because Hallie didn't necessarily know any of it either.

"I don't know what you need to do, but I'm going to do all I can to help you," Hallie said.

Sarah, of course, insisted on paying Hallie's going rate for her life coaching business. She didn't mind doing that because she had the money and knew she couldn't take advantage of her friend. Hallie didn't want to take the money from her, but Sarah sent it to her through VenMo and didn't let her argue about it.

The two women did some intense research on issues that Sarah needed to focus on and the steps that Sarah needed to take to throw her hat in the ring. And then they brainstormed about how to get the petition circulated.

When they got the logistics out of the way, it was time to figure out some more important issues. Namely, Sarah needed the confidence booster that she could do this. "I have to admit, I feel I'm out of my depth, and I need to get around the argument that people are going to make that I don't have an interest in the school board because I don't have a kid in school. And why am I running? I can't just be one note and say that I'm running to ensure books aren't banned."

Hallie nodded her head. "Well, the good news is that not everybody pays attention to these elections. I believe you just have to talk to enough people in the right areas to make sure that your name is on their lips when they enter the voting booth. So I think you should focus on the book banning issue, make sure the people know what books are being banned, why they're being banned, and why they shouldn't be. I think that's a good message to take to the community. It's really an awareness thing. A lot of parents you are going to be talking to probably don't even know what's going on. But many of them will be engaged, and you must make them see this is important."

So, for the rest of the evening, Hallie and Sarah studied the list of books that were proposed to be banned, which included Pulitzer Prize winners and classics. "I just can't believe that *To Kill a Mockingbird* would be on this list," Sarah said, shaking her head. "I can almost see the other books on this list, but not this one."

Hallie was helpful because she agreed to play Devil's Advocate so that Sarah would understand the arguments she might come in contact with. She needed to know the opposition to counter it.

"It's being banned because of the white Savior thing, the flagrant use of the N-word, and because it might increase racial tensions. The district is interested in not telling stories that might make African-Americans and white people have more conflict. And that's the same reason why Huck Finn is being banned and *Gone With the Wind*. Plus, *Gone With the Wind* might be interpreted as glorifying slavery because the servants who worked in the house were portrayed almost as if they were like family members or friends instead of slaves. Plus, *Gone With the Wind* portrays the KKK with sympathy."

Sarah wrote down the objections that Hallie verbalized in her role as Devil's Advocate and realized that all the arguments had a great deal of merit. "Okay, I understand where the parents concerned about these books are coming from. My proposal would be to integrate the books into the curriculum, so they could be the basis for thoughtful discussion on the racial themes in these books. Because students must be exposed to themes, but they shouldn't use the books as a basis to be discriminatory to other people."

"But what about the idea that the book should be available in the library and not integrated into the curriculum?"

"Well, to be realistic, not many kids of that age will pick up any of those books as pleasure reading. And the ones that will probably will be unusually bright and curious, and they can handle the themes in those books. And teachers can assign the books as extra credit, accompanied with a book report, and the teacher can engage the student in a discussion."

Hallie made a face. "Your argument isn't strong enough on this issue. I agree that these books should be integrated into the curriculum, studied, debated, and dissected. But the themes in these books might be a lot for young children to handle on their own."

Sarah wanted to protest that as she thought of Emerson and how thoughtful and intelligent the young girl was. "I don't agree. I think that the students in that school are smart enough to understand that-"

Hallie shook her head. "Not everybody is a young child with a genius I.Q. like our Emerson. There are a lot of minorities in the school, and some kids are growing up in households that are less than accepting of diversity. The themes might be hurtful to minorities and embolden the students who are learning discriminatory ideas from their parents. The books on this list might increase students' ideas about white supremacy. You have to take that into account."

Sarah saw Hallie's arguments and realized she might've been myopic about the entire thing. She was such a non-censorship and free speech absolutist that she wasn't considering how certain themes might affect young minds.

"I see your point. So maybe the solution is to integrate these books into the curriculum but take them out of the library. But I don't agree when it comes to books like *1984* and *The Great Gatsby*. Neither of those books particularly focuses on racial equity. They both are important works and are unlikely to be integrated into the curriculum, but they should be available to the kids."

"*1984* might be very disturbing to the young child because it does have such strong themes. And *The Great Gatsby* glorifies drinking and extramarital affairs." Hallie smiled. "And I personally think *The Great Gatsby* is very over-rated. I know it's considered a great American novel, but I can't imagine why."

Sarah felt she was on stronger ground in articulating why those two books should be available. "*1984* is a disturbing book with disturbing themes, but bright young students should have access to it. It imagines a world, ironically, where censorship is taken to its logical extension. It shows what dangers lurk when there are thought police and people are told how to think by the government. It's a cautionary tale that all students should be exposed to. As for *The Great Gatsby*, I agree with you. It's overrated. But I still think the themes are important in the book. Money doesn't buy happiness, and the characters were nihilists, none of whom were entirely happy. Perhaps the lesson in the book is that living an empty life devoid of values or care for your fellow man will lead to ruin. I think that's a good book to read. If students want to read it, they should be able to."

Hallie nodded her head. "Those are good reasons to keep the books in the library. You're right. 1984 is a good book because the school board is trying to exercise censor-ship. That book talks about what happens when censorship is the law of the land. But you have to be careful in thinking students can handle racist themes without a careful hand that would help them understand that, say, *Huckleberry Finn* is a satire that's meant to skewer the racist attitudes of the South in those days not glorify it. And *Gone With the Wind* is the perfect archetype of the Lost Cause theory of the confederacy and not a good depiction of the antebellum south."

"And *To Kill a Mockingbird?*" Sarah asked. She still thought that book should be available in the library.

"That's a closer call. But there's a big concern about the white Savior thing – that racism is best resolved by white people and not by those who belong to that particular race. And there are lots of problematic uses of the N-word in that book. Plus, it might inflame racial tension. That book should probably stay with the curriculum and not be widely available. But I definitely think it should be part of the curriculum. It's a very important book."

Sarah nodded her head. She felt she was getting a pretty good argument together to take on the road.

Hallie cocked her head. "Weren't you supposed to get expert help from some big shot guy involved in D.C. politics?" she asked.

"Yes, but that's a sore subject. He didn't want to take me on. I think he thinks I'm some kind of a radical or something like that. Imagine that, me, a radical. It's laughable."

Hallie smiled. "I think you have more of your mother's traits than you know. I remember Ava telling me about how your mother was a 60s activist in her day. I'm sure she'd cheer you on in this project if she knew about it."

"I'm sure she would be. But she's busy these days. She has a new love interest in her life. Barbara, who's a real hoot and is like mom in many ways."

"I'd love to meet this Barbara. Your mom is quite a card. I hope she's doing well."

"She is. She is. I love that she and Ava are so good now. That's all I ever wanted for them. Anyhow, Max Stein wants nothing to do with me."

Hallie scrunched up her eyebrows. "Oh, the guy who was going to take you on is named Max Stein? You know, I heard something about him. He owns a farm now, right?"

"Right."

Hallie nodded her head. "There's a story about why he's

here on this island. I've heard bits and pieces about it. Something about some tragedy happened with an adopted daughter of his. Anyhow, I don't know much about it. I just heard he moved here because something horrible happened in D.C."

"Oh. You don't remember what that was?"

"No. I just heard something about that because I was curious about why the guy who owns a great farm came here after living in a big city. It interested me because it has a lot of parallels with all of us. We all came from big cities, and now we're here. I know I'm much happier here than I was in New York City. Ava and Quinn are too. And Quinn is really happy to be raising a kid here instead of raising Emerson in a big city. And I think that's part of why he's here is because he wants to raise his daughter in a small town. But something else drove him out of D.C. You might ask him about that."

Sarah just grimaced. "I don't think I'm going to be talking to him. I went to his farm because I wanted to ask him about the campaign management thing, and he turned me down flat because he didn't like what I stood for. So that's that."

But, it turned out that wasn't necessarily that.

Sarah's phone rang. She didn't recognize the number, but it was a local number, so she picked it up.

It was Max Stein, asking for a meeting.

Chapter Ten

Ava

Ava nervously approached Christopher, who was sitting at a table with a view at The Straight Wharf. The beautiful restaurant overlooked the harbor, and the seats by the windows were the most coveted. But it was March, so it wasn't packed, but it definitely wasn't empty.

Ava wondered how Christopher managed to score such a prime seat.

She sat down, and Christopher stood and offered her his hand. Ava had a laugh at the gesture. They were married for 10 years, dating for five, and he acted like they had just met on Tinder and were meeting in person for the first time.

He was extremely nervous, and that was plain.

"I ordered your favorite wine and oysters. I know how much you always loved them."

Ava smiled reassuringly. "Actually, I've given up oysters. I did a test on food sensitivities, and it turned out that oysters ignite an inflammatory response in my body, so I've given them up. I've given up almonds for the same reason."

And that was true. Even though Ava, for the most part, had decided to eat cleanly, she still had some digestive upsets, and she didn't know what caused them. So she took a test, found out what foods she was sensitive to, and cut them out. Or, at least, as with gluten, she limited them. She still ate pizza with her ladies weekly, but that was the exception. But, in the case of the oysters, she cut them out completely because it turned out she was highly sensitive to them.

Christopher's face looked crestfallen after she told him she couldn't eat the oysters. "I'm sorry. I should've asked you, but I remember how much you always loved eating them with me. I guess I'm still living in the past in a way."

Ava touched Christopher's arm. "Don't worry about it. You obviously don't know much about my life these days, and I don't know much about yours."

She looked at the menu and decided on the salmon dish. It was served with arugula, roasted beets, and a type of wild mushroom called "hen of the woods." It was one of her favorite things on the menu.

"Okay, I know what I want to eat. So let's just order, and we can catch up."

The waitress came around, took their order, and delivered the oysters. Christopher sheepishly ate them all on his own.

"I'm embarrassed. I should know more about you than I do."

Ava shook her head. "How could you know anything about me? You've been gone for the past two years. Before that, we weren't on the same page about anything for at least five years. Not that I understand why, but it was what was."

Christopher took a deep breath. "You remember my parents, don't you?"

Ava remembered his parents very well. Unfortunately. Chris' wealthy father, Bill, who was from South Carolina, was a big strapping man who used to play college football, still used terms like "little lady," and casually used racial slurs in everyday conversation. Ava disliked him immensely, especially after, when he met her for the first time, he told Christopher that he thought "she'd be thinner." That was all he said about her - she was apparently too pudgy for Bill O'Neill's taste. He didn't have anything to say about her graduating from Harvard Law, her sense of humor, or her love for his son. Just that she was too fat.

His mother, a former beauty queen, was a complete snob who obviously looked at Ava and found her lacking. She couldn't be more unfriendly if she tried.

Ava spent one uncomfortable week with Christopher's parents in Virginia over one terrible Christmas holiday and swore she would never do that again.

"Yes. I do remember your parents."

"Well, there's something I didn't tell you about my dad. Actually, a couple of things. And one of the things is my sister accused him of molesting her when she was young."

Ava buttered her bread as she listened to Christopher. This was bombshell news, although it wasn't entirely shocking. His father struck her as somebody who'd do something like that.

"She accused him. Did you believe her? Did your mother?" She hoped the answer to those questions would be "yes," but maybe not. Ava thought that that kind of accusation wouldn't be created out of thin air. But then again, families who experienced that type of thing didn't like talking about it and often lived in denial. Especially if there was no hope of the parents divorcing. The mother in the family would have to live in denial if she would stay with the father if he did that type of thing.

"No. For the longest time, I didn't. That was why I quit talking to her. But I never told you that. I just said we were estranged because we didn't get along. I just didn't tell you why we didn't get along."

"What changed your mind?" Ava asked.

"My father's suicide." He bit his bottom lip. "It happened about five years ago."

Five years ago. That was about when Christopher started to pull away. "Your father committed suicide, and you never told me?" Ava asked.

"Yes. I never even told you he was dead. I was so ashamed he'd kill himself. And I was embarrassed because a part of me always believed my sister. And, after he died, my mom admitted that she believed my sister too."

"She believed your sister? Did she always believe her? Or did she just decide to believe her because her father committed suicide, and maybe he put it in his note? A full confession in his note."

"No. There was no full confession. But mom told me she felt imprisoned by my father and couldn't leave him. So, because she felt trapped in the marriage, she had to take his side against my sister."

Ava took a sip of her wine, which had just arrived at the table. "Why was she trapped?"

"He apparently threatened her life. He beat her. I never told you about any of that. My family was so dysfunctional, so full of secrets and lies, and I was ashamed of all of it. That was why I never subjected you to them after that one week from hell that you spent with them in Virginia."

"How awful. And I'm so sorry you couldn't talk to me about this. You just kept all that in."

He nodded his head. "Yes. And I hated him after I found all this out. But I stopped hating him after finding out at least part of why he acted the way he did. He was diagnosed with bipolar disorder when he was 13 years old. He suffered from delusions at that time and was confined to a mental hospital for six months. Again, that was something my mom recently told me."

"It sounded like your mom opened the vault after he died."

"And how. All of a sudden, a lot of things made sense. My dad refused to take any kind of meds for his bipolar disorder. When he was younger, he was in and out of the mental ward. But when he became an adult and nobody could force him to take meds or go into the hospital, he decided to pretend he wasn't ill. So his sickness came out in other ways. He drank, abused my mom, molested my sister, and acted like a total jerk his entire life."

Ava narrowed her eyes. "Any chance you inherited his genes?" That would explain so much. One of the hallmarks of mania, which was one of the poles in bipolar disorder, the other one being depression, was that people in the throes of mania did things like indiscriminately have sex with strangers, spend a lot of money, stay up for days on end and talk incessantly, feel they were King of the world, and take a lot of risks.

And gamble. That was definitely an action that manic people took.

"Yes. I inherited his genes. And I took meds when I was young. My mother took me to the doctor when I was very young. She saw the signs of bipolar, and I was put on meds when I was nine. I never told you that, either."

One thing was for sure. This dinner was turning out to be revelatory. Much more so than Ava had ever anticipated. "So, you were on meds your whole life for bipolar?"

"No. I didn't like the way the meds made me feel. My emotions were flattened. My creativity was gone. The kitchen could be on fire, and I would just let it burn. And I was like my dad, living in denial about it. I never wanted to admit I had a problem. I thought it showed weakness. And there's a social stigma around the term 'mental illness.' You hear the term mental illness, and you think about homeless people and people who hear voices and warn people aliens are about to land. And I also felt I did my job better when I wasn't taking meds. I had so much energy for my job, such clear thinking, and I had such a killer attitude when I was manic."

Christopher's story was hitting home with Ava. She thought many people, but men especially, never wanted to admit to having a mental problem. And she could understand that Christopher, with a high-powered banking job, probably welcomed the excess energy he got when on the high-end of the bipolar scale.

Ava nodded her head. "I know a little bit about mental illness. And I'd imagine your father's suicide probably sent you over the edge."

"Yes. It did. But it led me to other things, something else that really sent me over the edge. But I still can't talk to you about that. I'm sorry. But, yes, I definitely self-destructed at that point."

"Christopher, you can tell me anything. You don't need to hide anything from me anymore." She wanted to add that he didn't need to hide anything from her because she didn't care anymore about anything he did during their marriage. But she felt that that would just be piling on, so she kept her mouth shut.

"No. I can't talk about it right now. Anyhow, my father's suicide really kicked my mania into overdrive. And the gambling thing really fed on itself. It's the worst addiction you can ask for because it all just feeds on itself. I went to the tables because I was manic and wanted to take risks. And when I started to lose, I swung into depression. The more I lost, the more I felt worthless about myself. And the more determined I got to win it all back."

"It's a vicious circle, gambling," Ava said. She knew something about sunk costs, where you lose so much you can't walk away. Sunk costs were why the United States stayed in Vietnam for so long - so many men had died or been permanently maimed, and so much money was spent in the conflict that the country couldn't get out of the war. Gambling was much the same on a much smaller scale - at some point, you feel you have to keep going because if you don't, all those losses will be for naught.

"Right. Because you get so down and you've lost so much money. You always think your jackpot, the big pot of money that'll bring you to square one, is just around the corner. But of course, it never is. You just keep getting further and further into the hole. At some point, you get desperate. Which was what I was when I took all that money from you. I owed over $1 million to some Chinese gangsters from Macau."

Ava sat across from the man who had so fundamentally betrayed her, and she had to feel just a bit sorry for him. "How did you get millions in debt?" Ava had never even heard of that type of thing. She'd heard of high rollers and people getting in over their heads. She'd heard of casinos giving their highest rollers gambling markers, which was an advance. She'd heard of gamblers being indebted to loan sharks.

But she'd never heard of people who owed Chinese gangsters over $1 million.

"You're naïve if you don't know how that can happen. It happens. It happened to a Swiss priest, who found himself over $1 million in debt, so he took money from his parishioners to cover it. The highest rollers can lose $30-40 million on gambling. And you don't know the high it is to be in a private VIP gambling room in Macau with some of the wealthiest and highest rollers in the entire world. You can smell the money in those places. And winning hands against these guys, there's nothing like it. It gave me a serotonin rush like nothing else."

Ava narrowed her eyes. Something wasn't jibing. "Christopher, how did you get invited to these super high roller rooms? You weren't a billionaire. How did you get invited to places where billionaires were playing?"

Christopher cleared his throat and didn't meet Ava's eyes. "I'd rather not talk about that. And don't press me on it because I'm not going to tell you. But I will tell you there was no bigger rush than playing with these guys. No bigger rush than winning a hundred thousand dollars on one hand. One hand!"

He smiled as if thinking about that day in the sun when he apparently won a hundred thousand dollars in one hand of poker.

"I had a straight flush. The fellow across the table from me, who was such a big name that even you would know who he was, had four aces. He thought nobody could beat him, and I don't blame him for feeling that way. You have four aces. You're going to win 99.999999% of the time. It was a dream scenario. Having a straight flush when someone else at the table has four aces? You just know you'll win a lot of money with those facts."

Ava buttered her bread and took a sip of her wine. "And I imagine that the perks were fantastic. I'm sure you got much more from these casinos and hotels than free buffets, am I right?"

"Oh, yes. Penthouse suites comped. Bottles of Dom Perignon sent to your table for free. You never have to pay for a meal anywhere. In Macau, high rollers are even given prostitutes for free. Drugs, if you want them. I didn't take them up on the prostitute or drugs offer, but I loved staying in the penthouse suites of these places."

Ava imagined Christopher was seduced by the glamour of the casinos' penthouses, the high of winning big hands, and the applause of people when you win big in one of those high-roller casinos.

"Okay. So, I guess I understand a little bit about why you did what you did. How did you get the money back? You obviously did."

Christopher nervously took a sip of his whiskey sour, and his hand shook. "I don't want to get into that."

So many unanswered questions. While Ava was happy she was drilling down into some of the things Christopher needed to talk to her about, she realized there was much more to the story than he was willing to tell her.

"Okay. You lost millions at the gambling tables in Macau. What brings you here? Besides me, of course."

"My sister married somebody who lives on the island. She's divorcing him and needs me to help her escape her toxic relationship."

"What kind of help are you getting her?"

"Moral support, mainly. Ava, I was terrible to her when

she made the accusations against our father. I shunned her. I didn't believe her. I made her feel she wasn't welcome at our gatherings. But when my mom finally told me she believed Nicole's story and that my father had confided in her the story was true, I felt awful. I never should've had such a knee-jerk reaction. I always should've listened to her, at the very least. But I didn't. And now I have a lot of making up to do with her. To say the very least. I owe her this time. So I'm staying at the Wauwinet and will stay there until the divorce is finalized. She's staying there with me."

Ava took a deep breath. Again, there was something he wasn't telling her. It made a little sense that he would be staying on the island for his sister, but at the same time, there was something else. She could see it in his eyes. She knew her ex-husband like the back of her hand. She wasn't surprised he was a bad gambler because he always had a terrible poker face.

"That's nice. Now tell me the real reason why you're here."

He didn't look at her but kept looking in his wineglass as if he was looking for the answer to her question at the bottom of that glass. "Ava, I don't know what you're talking about. I'm here for Nicole."

"You're here for your sister." She shook her head. "Listen, Chris, I'm happy you've come clean on the dark secrets of your family, but I wish you would just implicate yourself. You're not a victim. You're certainly not an angel. Yet you're trying to come off as both of those things, and I can't figure out why."

"I don't know what you're talking about."

"Don't you? So far, I've only gotten half-truths and outright lies." The waiter brought their food around, and Ava dug into her salmon. "Why do I even care? You paid me back the money. That's all you're obligated to do. You're still hiding and lying, which means we can't even be friends."

"Ava, I'm not lying."

"Bullshit," Ava said. "Don't even try to tell me you're not up to no good because I know you are. I don't know exactly what you're involved with, but I know it's something."

At that, Chris put a phone number on a slip of paper. "Here. This is my sister's phone number. You can call her. She'll tell you I've been staying with her at the hotel, helping her emotionally with her divorce."

Ava took the phone number. "I will call her."

He shook his head. "You never trusted me."

"Do you blame me? Look at what you did. Listen, I know you had a hard life, and you were dealt a bad hand with your mental illness. Pardon the expression. And I'm sorry to hear about your father. I'd imagine having something like that in your family is hard to stomach, to say the least. But you had a choice, and you made the wrong one."

"What choice?"

"You had a choice to take meds for your bipolar disorder. You had a choice to tell me about what was going on with your family. You had a choice to go to therapy to deal with your feelings about your father. You took none of those paths. Instead, you robbed me blind, took off without a word and without telling me where you would be. I'm happy you finally decided to tell me a little about why you did what you did, but we can't be friends until you come clean with me about the rest."

He looked pained. "This isn't how I thought it was going to go," he said. "I really thought we could be on good terms."

Ava took a deep breath. "Chris, we can be friendly.

There's no reason not to be. But I really want you to come clean. There's something gigantic you're not telling me. But that's okay. I really don't care. But I'm concerned about the money you gave me. I think it's dirty, and I'm not going to touch it."

"Why do you think it's dirty?"

"Because I do. Because you haven't told me yet you've been working. So, if you're not working, how did you get that kind of money? That's what I need to know."

"Ava, have you ever known me to do anything dirty? Anything illegal?"

"No. But you've been hiding things all along in our marriage, apparently. How do I know you haven't been hiding something else that's much more dark and sinister? Besides, you borrowed from Chinese gangsters. You're capable of anything."

Chris hesitated, but then he shook his head. "I guess I'll have to prove myself to you again."

"Why? I don't understand why you want to prove yourself to me and work to get on my good side. There's zero chance we'll ever get back together. Why is it so important to prove yourself to me?"

"Because I don't want you to hate me. I want us to be on good terms. I miss you, and I miss the kids. I know the kids are only my stepkids, but I got quite attached to them. I've wondered how they are."

Ava felt she was on much more sturdy ground talking about the kids. She was grateful for that. "They're doing smashing, all of them. Even Samantha. Actually, especially Samantha." Ava chuckled a little. "It's so crazy. My flighty daughter, the one I was worried about because she always seemed to be spinning her wheels and going nowhere, has turned out to be the most successful and stable of all of them."

Chris had a gleam in his eye. It seemed he was genuinely interested in the kids. He was always close with them, and they were always close with him. "Samantha, a success? Who knew?"

"I know! I thought for sure she'd be the one that would give me stomach ulcers from all the stress. But she's involved in a very stable relationship with Grayson. And she's one of the most sought-after cake designers on the island."

"Grayson, huh? I wondered when she would realize he was the one for her. I always liked that kid. What about the others? Did Jackson ever make it big in Hollywood? I keep thinking I'll see his name on a movie poster one day."

"Not yet. But, it's only a matter of time. I really believe that. Not that I'm not nervous every day for him. He's in such a dog-eat-dog world. But he has the mental toughness to make it. As for Charlotte, she seems to be doing pretty good. She's working as a ghostwriter for an artist who also is a novelist. His name is Conrad, and he writes historical fiction. She's working on a novel for him. And I think she's doing well with her marriage."

Actually, Ava worried Charlotte was still on thin ice with Matthew. They broke up for a while because Matthew didn't want a family. But they got back together when their small baby, Siobhan, almost died. But Ava couldn't help but be worried that only a Band-Aid was put on their marriage, a reprieve from the inevitable.

Christopher genuinely looked like he was happy to be hearing about the kids. "I really hope Jackson sets the world on fire. He deserves it. He's such a good kid. And I'm so happy that Sam is doing so well!"

"Well, Sam is living on the island. I'll have to talk to her and see if she's okay with you getting in touch with her, but I think she will be, knowing Sam. She always sees the best in people and never holds a grudge. She's my sweet butterfly of a daughter."

"I'd love to talk to her, one on one. So yes, if you don't mind asking her if she doesn't mind seeing me, I'd like to give her a call and meet with her sometime. So, she's a really good cake designer?"

"She's amazing. I never even knew she had it in her. I always assumed she would be one of those kids who would drift along in life. I assumed she would end up moving in with me at some point. But she surprised me."

"You should be proud. It sounds like you did a great job with those kids."

"Thanks. I'm surprised they turned out as well as they did. And, you know, this is only a snapshot in time. Jackson's future is far from certain. So is Charlotte's, for that matter. Neither of them seem all that settled. But they're not into drugs, and they don't seem to have any kind of bad habits that might lead them to ruin. So I guess that's a win."

"A win, for sure," Christopher said. And then he looked sad. "I wish I would have had children with you. Or had children at all. It's great hearing about the stepkids, but they're not legally obligated to be in my life. And whether or not they talk to me is completely up to you. So it's not the same as having biological children."

Of course, when Ava and Christopher married, it was agreed they'd have no more children. Having three children at home was more than enough, they agreed.

"Chris, you helped raise them. And you were always good about being in their lives. I'll give you that."

Ava still didn't trust the man. How could she? He hid so much from her during their marriage, and he apparently was still hiding things now. But that had nothing to do with the kids. And she knew Samantha, at least, missed him. It was hard on Samantha not having a father figure in her life. And for the duration of their marriage, Chris was their father figure.

Jackson and Charlotte also craved the masculine energy Chris brought to the home. But Jackson was across the country, so she didn't think Chris and Jackson would probably hang out and try to get to know one another again. Charlotte was in Boston, so she was a lot closer. But Charlotte was always a tough nut to crack, and she had a lot going on in her life. So Ava doubted Charlotte would be interested in a reunion with Chris.

Ava and Chris ordered dessert, and, over crème brûlées, they talked about everything under the sun.

Chapter Eleven

Sarah

Sarah nervously waited to talk to Max. They had arranged to meet at Lola's for some sushi. Sarah got there a little early and ordered a glass of sake. She had no idea why she was nervous about meeting this guy. She only knew she was.

About 7 o'clock, he arrived. He was actually smiling, which was a bit of an odd thing to see for Sarah. Usually, when she was in his presence, he was frowning. The smile gave him a bit of a boyish look. With his dark curly hair and dimples, he looked just a bit like a young Tom Hanks during the days when he played a man in drag in the television show *Bosom Buddies*. Sarah used to watch that show when she was very young, and she was amazed at the career Tom Hanks managed to wrangle after such an inauspicious start.

"Have you been waiting here long?" he asked her as he sat down.

Sarah shook her head. "No, actually. I just got here. I'm glad you suggested this place because I love the food here."

He nodded his head. "Me too. Okay, let's forget about the small talk. I suppose you're wondering what made me change my mind about talking to you."

"I admit, I'm curious. You were so adamant before about not wanting me as a client. What made you change your mind?"

He smiled again, which put Sarah just a little bit off balance. "I don't really know. I talked to Julia, and she put me in my place, as only a young teenager can. She told me I was being ridiculous, or redic, as the kids say, and I never turned away from a fight before." And then he appeared to take a deep breath. "And I have very personal reasons for not wanting to represent you before. But I decided to use my rational brain instead of my emotions. And I thought I might actually try to hear you out."

Sarah wondered what the personal reasons were. "So, there's something that you've experienced that makes you want to not have an open mind about the book censorship?"

"Yes." But that was all he said, and it was clear that he wouldn't say more. So Sarah decided not to press him.

"So, you said you wanted to hear me out. What do you want to ask me?"

"Well, I got the impression the other night when you were speaking to the school board that you were talking off the cuff. Like you hadn't really researched the issues so much."

That was actually true. Sarah didn't research the book banning thing before speaking her piece at the school board meeting. It was more of a visceral, gut reaction to the injustice of censoring classic books. And if there was one thing Sarah was against, it was injustice.

She was always on the side of the underdog. Even when she was in high school and considered the most popular girl in school, she stood up for people being bullied. She used her popularity to stick up for marginalized people. One of her best friends in high school was a young girl named Jamie, who had Down's Syndrome. Woe to anybody who tried to insult Jamie - Sarah would cut them where they stood, and her popularity meant her words were taken seriously.

Sarah felt these books were suffering a kind of injustice. They all had something important to say, but they were essentially being bullied into nonexistence, which bothered Sarah. It came down to Sarah's belief that the powerful too often tried to squash the little guy and the defenseless. And, in this case, these books were the defenseless ones. They were inanimate objects, which rendered them at the complete mercy of people who profess to know better than anybody else about whether or not they're appropriate.

Sarah cleared her throat. "You're right. I went to the school board that evening because Emerson urged me to. And I really decided to run for the school board on the fly." Sarah didn't want to tell Max he was part of why she decided to run for the school board. He made her so angry that night that she wanted to run for the board just to show him.

"That's what I thought. And I wanted to meet with you to see if you'd done the research and if maybe you've reached a more nuanced position."

"Yes, I think I have." And then Sarah proceeded to tell Max what she thought. She told him that she thought some of the more racially sensitive books needed to be in the curriculum but didn't necessarily belong in the school library.

Max listened to her words and nodded along. "That's an interesting point of view. Many parents would say the opposite – don't make them mandatory reading, and don't put them into the curriculum, but keep them in the library."

"I'm on the fence about that, actually. I know the arguments, and I must admit they're not too much out in left field. But I would hate to live in a world where our middle schoolers are deprived of the words of Atticus Finch or Scarlett O'Hara. Or Huck Finn."

The waiter came around, and Sarah ordered a rainbow roll and seaweed salad, while Max ordered a dragon roll and a crunch roll with a side of mixed sashimi.

"I know what you're saying. And I agree, for the most part. But, at the same time, I don't want our young children exposed to certain things. We should let them have a childhood before they're forced to deal with racial hatred and bigotry."

Sarah sat back. "So, maybe we're a bit on the same page," she said.

"Maybe. At first, I thought you were some kind of First Amendment absolutist who thought our kids should be exposed to anything and everything in the library."

Sarah had a laugh about that one. "No. Even I would object to *Playboy* sharing space with *Time* magazine on a middle school shelf. And I definitely am not on board with our young kids having easy access to *Fifty Shades of Grey.* There should always be limits."

Max bit his lower lip. "Okay. Maybe you want my consulting work. And that's all it's going to be - consultation. I decided to stop running campaigns. But I can be available to you to advise you on how to approach your campaign. You need to know the nuts and bolts, but you also need to know how to fundraise, talk to people, and find volunteers. I can help with all that."

Sarah was a bit disappointed. She wanted him to tell her

that he would run her campaign. But, if she could get consultation from a D.C.-level pro, that was the next best thing.

"I'd like that. What's your going rate?"

He shrugged his shoulders. "One hundred dollars an hour. I usually charge more than that, but my past Nantucket clients have always been running for something more substantial than the school board. They're usually running for state Senate or House. I don't do national clients anymore, of course."

"That's a reasonable rate," Sarah said, nodding. "When do we get started?"

"We can get started tomorrow if you like. I'm assuming you don't have a campaign office?"

"You assume correctly. I'm going to be working out of my house for now. I don't know how big of an operation I want this to be just yet."

"That's understandable. And smart."

They finished their dinner and finalized the plans for him to come over to her house at 7:30 the next evening.

Chapter Twelve

Ava

Ava called her daughters and son to tell them the news about Christopher. Charlotte was indignant that Ava would even speak to the man after what he did. Jackson was his usual self – casual about the whole thing. He told her he was happy for her because maybe she needed to close the door on him. And he said he wouldn't judge Chris because he never walked a mile in Chris's shoes.

His reaction was so like Jackson, giving everybody the benefit of the doubt. He was so opposite of Charlotte, who was stubborn and hardheaded and could be so closed-minded.

As for Samantha, she squealed with delight when Ava called her about Chris. "Mom, that's great!" she said excit-edly. "I never thought Chris was a bad guy. I always thought he had a lot of sadness and felt sorry for him."

And that was so Samantha. Samantha, out of all her kids, had the most empathy for people. She sometimes could be very self-centered, and she used to be quite flighty, but she always felt the emotions of people who were struggling mentally.

"Well, he's on the island. I guess he's going to be here indefinitely. So, if you'd like to talk to him, I could put you guys in touch."

"Mom, I'd love that. When do you want to meet?"

"Well, I know you have a busy schedule. So, whenever you can make it. I'm pretty open, and I think Chris is as well."

"He's not working?"

"No. I don't think he is."

"So how is he staying on this island? Where does he have the money for that Wauwinet place? I know that place is high dollar."

Ava had to admit that she didn't know the answer to that question. She asked it herself in her head. It was one of many gaps in Chris's story.

"Maybe his sister has money?"

"Maybe. That's probably it. Anyhow, mom, let's meet tomorrow night. I actually can't wait to see him."

The next evening, Ava hosted Samantha and Chris at the house. And she invited Jessica to have dinner with them as well. After all, Jessica seemed to know Chris. And, at this point, Jessica probably knew more about Chris than she did. That was the nature of the AA confessionals – they encouraged their members to be honest.

But if Jessica knew Chris's secrets, she didn't let on. But she did tell Ava that she didn't feel comfortable hanging out with Ava's husband. "It's hard to separate him from the

Chris I know at the meetings. We're all metaphorically stripped naked during those meetings. That's very important for our recoveries. But it's just a tad embarrassing in a social setting, knowing what you know about the other person and what that person knows about you."

Ava nodded her head. "That's understandable. I probably would be the same way."

"Just know he's trying very hard to recover and become a better person. I'm glad you're giving him a chance."

Ava made a face. "I am giving him a chance. I'm giving him a chance to re-establish a relationship with Samantha and possibly become friendly with me. But I don't see us becoming true friends, and I really don't see us getting involved romantically."

"Well, keep an open mind. But thanks for the invitation. Maybe some other time."

So, Ava found herself on her deck, listening to the waves, and thinking about her relationship with Chris. It wasn't something she'd cared to rehash in the wake of his betrayal. She didn't like to dwell on what happened because it made her feel like a failure. She was a victim because he stole all that money, and she didn't like to dwell on that, either. She hated thinking of herself as either a victim or a failure, let alone both, which was what she was in this situation.

But now he was here, and she was forced to deal with it, which meant she had to think of her role in the entire situation. Where did she go wrong? *Did* she go wrong? Yes, of course, she did at some point. If she didn't, everything would've worked out.

Wouldn't it have?

But then she thought about what Chris had told her about his family. And how he kept it secret from her the entire time. Perhaps it was none of her business what kind of lowlifes Chris had in his family. But it affected her because that apparently caused Chris to pull away. So, it would've helped if he had been straight with her. Or straight with their marital therapist. Or with anybody.

She supposed it was a good sign that he was now being honest. She didn't really know why he decided to now be honest with her, but she thought it might have some to do with his 12-step meetings. Perhaps telling his stories to the strangers at those meetings broke the ice for him. It made him realize he could say those words to another person, and the sky didn't fall.

Perhaps he took the first steps towards bravery, and he liked it. So he decided to take the next step and come clean to her.

Samantha arrived. She ran and hugged Ava and then took off her coat as soon as she got under the heat lamp. "Mom, have I told you how smart it was to get these heat lamps? It's colder than a witch's tit out there, but I stand under these heat lamps, and it's like the Bahamas."

Ava smiled as she offered Samantha a glass of wine, and her daughter eagerly accepted. "Yes, please. Especially if it's wine Aunt Sarah bought. She really knows her stuff."

After Ava poured the wine, Samantha took a sip and nodded. "Yep. That's definitely wine Aunt Sarah bought. It's very good."

"That it is," Ava agreed.

"So, what exactly is going on with Chris? I told Grayson about him appearing out of nowhere, and Grayson thought it was weird. I don't know, I really don't know what to think. But it seems kinda odd."

"You're not having second thoughts about talking to him, are you?"

Samantha shrugged. "No. I was really excited about meeting him again. But Charlotte really thought I shouldn't talk to him. She told me I was being disloyal to you by being friendly with him."

"How did she work that out?" Ava asked. "I'm the one encouraging you to talk to him. It's not like you're going behind my back and meeting with him."

Sometimes Charlotte could be just so rigid.

Chris came up to the porch, and Ava went down to greet him. She led him up to the roof terrace, where he saw Samantha and awkwardly smiled at her. He stood there as if he didn't know what to do, which was probably the case.

All at once, Ava's heart went out to him. She could see his awkwardness, his nervousness about seeing his step-daughter again. It was written all over his face that he wanted her acceptance but was terrified he wouldn't get it.

But Samantha, true to form, dispelled all doubts as she went over to him and gave him a big hug. He hugged her back, tears in his eyes.

"Look at you," he said to her. "You look so radiant like you have this light shining out through your eyes. You must be happy."

"Insanely! I mean, I have the greatest guy in the world at home. And I have my dream job. Life couldn't be better, especially after all the wheel spinning I did before this. It's funny how life can settle when you stop fighting things you can't change."

Ava thought Samantha was being wise with her words. Ava never imagined that Samantha would be the one to have insight, but she apparently was maturing.

"Yes, you're right about that," Chris said. "At some point, you just have to stop trying to swim upstream and let go. And then, when you do that, you find your true path."

Samantha glanced over at Ava. "And your true path, Chris, brought you here?"

Chris just nodded his head. As Ava looked at his face, she saw something unspoken. But it was hard to imagine what that thing might've been.

But Samantha didn't notice any artifice in Chris's face, so Ava let it go. Ava might've imagined the look, maybe misinterpreting it, but she doubted it. She knew him too well.

"Well, I'm glad you're here," Samantha said. "I've always wondered about you. Even when stupid Charlotte was making you out to be the devil himself, I always said there was more to the story."

Chris chuckled slightly when Samantha said there was more to the story. "Oh, trust me, there's always more to the story. Your mother can fill you in on things I was going through when I left."

Samantha, Chris, and Ava had a pleasant enough dinner. Samantha excitedly told him about the weddings and events she'd been working on, designing and creating the most beautiful cakes imaginable. She had an Instagram page dedicated to her cakes, and she had quite a few followers – 10,590, to be exact. And she gained all the followers within the last few months, as her name was being bandied about by wealthy influential people.

On her Instagram page were engaged people complimenting her cakes and talking about them. With every picture she posted, she had thousands of likes and hundreds of comments.

"I never could've dreamed I'd be here less than a year ago. I was working three jobs, including Door Dash, and I was hunting for a wealthy guy to take care of me. It all worked out how it was supposed to," Samantha gushed. "I know you and mom always thought I'd end up on skid row or something, but things have taken off, and I couldn't be happier."

Ava could see her ex-husband's face swell with pride as Samantha spoke to Christopher. He helped raise Samantha, so her triumph was partially his as well.

And he was the one who told Ava about Samantha's artistic talent – she used to do sketches as doodles that were quite good. Chris saw the sketches and tried encouraging Samantha to pursue some kind of artistic endeavor. He suggested that she go to college for graphic arts or even advertising, but Samantha didn't do either. Ava knew Samantha never believed in herself, so when Chris told her she had artistic talent, she didn't take it seriously. And she wasn't serious about going to college, anyway. So, Samantha ignored Christopher's advice and chose to not go to college and to work at a bakery.

And as Ava thought about Chris and his encouragement of Samantha's artistic gifts, she also thought about how he was with her other two children. He might've pulled away from the marriage, but he always did engage with the kids. Not having children of his own and apparently always regretting that decision, Chris was looking to be a father figure. He found it with her three children.

There was the weekend that he helped Jackson move into his apartment in Los Angeles. He rented a U-Haul because Jackson couldn't afford to rent one on his own - Jackson was only 18 years old when he moved to Los Angeles and had just graduated from high school. Christopher encouraged Jackson's ambitions as well. Chris was the one who encouraged Jackson to try for modeling jobs while he waited for the inevitable acting career that was just on the horizon. Chris also helped Jackson find an agent. He knew quite a few agents in Los Angeles through his banking job because he had wealthy, influential clients who had access to the power brokers in the modeling world.

And Chris always attended Jackson's football and base-ball games and cheered him on when Jackson had piano recitals. He made time for Jackson, recognizing that he was the only male figure in Jackson's life. The boy needed to fill the void left by the death of his biological father, Daniel.

Chris always made time for Charlotte, as well. When she had boy trouble, she went to him because she wanted a man's perspective on it all. He listened to her and gave her advice. He was there for her when she went through the trauma of having the entire school whisper about her because she allegedly had slept with the head cheerleader's boyfriend. She was a virgin and extremely upset about the loose talk. Chris listened to her and gave her advice about that as well.

When Charlotte was applying to colleges, he helped her with the applications and the essays. He even talked to the admissions board for Cornell because he had connections on the board. That was one thing he supplied to the kids – he had a lot of connections because his job put him in touch with so many wealthy and influential people.

Charlotte was never aware of Chris's machinations behind the scenes when it came to her getting into Cornell, and she never would. Chris and Ava agreed never to tell her she wasn't entirely responsible for getting into the Ivy League school.

After a few minutes, Chris acted much less nervous around Samantha, and soon they talked as if they had never been estranged from each other. Samantha asked Chris a million questions about where he'd been, being careful not to directly address the fact that he stole so much money from Ava. He simply told her he'd been living in Paris and left it at that.

The three sat on the terrace for the rest of the evening, finally breaking up at 1 o'clock in the morning. By the time they all said good night, they were laughing, joking, and sharing stories.

And Ava was very confused about where her feelings stood regarding Christopher. She hadn't thought of him much in the past few years, preferring to just chalk up her relationship with him as a lapse in judgment that she would never repeat. It was easy to do because he wasn't around, and the story she created in her head featured mainly the bad times and not the good. She needed to focus on the negative because it helped her get over him. Now, here he was, and she was reminded of why she fell in love with him in the first place. He was funny, he listened, he was intelligent and cultured, and he truly adored the kids.

And, just like that, Ava allowed a flicker of feelings for the man. But only a flicker.

One thing was for sure, though. She could no longer compartmentalize Christopher. He was no longer in a pocket in her brain, stored away from her everyday existence. He was living and breathing, and his good qualities shined through.

When she went to bed that night, she thought that maybe, just maybe, she could allow Christopher back in her life.

But only as a friend.

Chapter Thirteen

Sarah

Max came over the next evening so he could help Sarah with getting her campaign underway. She greeted him at the door of her house, and he joined her at the kitchen table, where she was camping out with her laptop. Emerson was also there because Quinn had a business dinner with a potential client. Emerson, being 13 years old, of course could stay in her own house without supervision. However, Emerson usually liked to come over to Sarah's when she didn't have anything going on, and Quinn wasn't around. Sarah actually loved the company, and she thought Emerson might be just a little bit lonely, so the arrangement benefited both of them.

Of course, Emerson still wasn't thrilled that Sarah was getting friendly with Max. "Dude, if anybody talked to me the way that jerk talked to you that night, they'd be dead to me. But you do you."

So, when Max came over, Emerson gave him the stink

eye and refused to shake his hand when he offered it to her. "I'm good," she said pointedly to him.

Unlike Sarah, Emerson had some very black-and-white thinking when it came to the issue of censorship. To her, it was simply wrong that any book would be banned from the library.

"Sarah," she had said about the whole issue. "Everybody in my school sees much worse on Twitter than the language in these books. There's no putting that horse back in the barn, so if you get rid of these books, you won't be shielding our virgin eyes from anything. All you're doing is making sure kids my age are even dumber and more ignorant than we already are. And, trust me, a lot of kids my age are very dumb and ignorant."

And to prove the point, Emerson showed Sarah just a sampling of the messages she had seen on Twitter. There were racist tweets that used the N-word prodigiously, tweets that talked about violence, and tweets that had embedded videos of people engaging in sex acts. Facebook was much the same.

It was an eye-opening experience for Sarah, who was on Twitter and Facebook herself but had never been exposed to the kinds of tweets and Facebook posts that Emerson apparently had been exposed to.

"Why is all this stuff allowed?" Sarah asked.

"Because the world is apparently a cesspool, and people are going nuts out there. You don't know how much hate there is out there. So Twitter and Facebook can't keep up with the vileness of it all."

Max stood there with a goofy grin, obviously uncomfortable by Emerson's less-than-enthusiastic greeting. "Okay, let's get started."

"You're a Trojan horse," Emerson said with her arms

crossed. "And yes, I know what that means. I took AP Greek literature last year. All those soldier dudes flattening the city. And those Trojans were just dumber than a box of rocks for falling for it." And then she pointedly looked at Sarah.

Now, this was a new one. Emerson didn't tell Sarah before Max got there that she thought Max would try to sabotage her. Then again, he did change his mind in a hurry. And he didn't give a good reason for changing his mind. Still, Emerson apparently came up with this theory without consulting Sarah, and Sarah was annoyed.

"Emerson," she admonished her young charge. "I don't know what you're talking about."

She simply raised an eyebrow at Max, who looked embarrassed.

"You've been talking to Julia," he said to Emerson.

"You bet your sweet patootie," she said to Max. "And she told me Sarah needs to tell you to take a long walk off a short pier. She doesn't trust you, and neither do I."

Max nodded his head. "That's understandable. Julia and I have clashed a lot since we moved here. It's been hard, bringing her up on my own."

All at once, Sarah's heart went out to him. "Yes, I can imagine it was." She was confused, though, about Julia. After all, Julia was the one who recommended her dad to Sarah. What made her change her mind? Or maybe she didn't change her mind, but Emerson was lying. For whatever reason.

She also wondered what happened to Julia's mom. Were they divorced? Did she die? Sarah thought it was probably the latter because of the sad look on his face. She probably passed away somehow. She couldn't imagine something like that happening to someone she loved. Her boyfriend in Monterey, Nolan, died after she spent over two decades with him. But that was different. She secretly despised him for many years, so his death didn't sadden her like it should have. And the fact that his death didn't send her into a state of grief ironically caused her a great deal of grief. And questioning.

"Julia tells me you won't take anybody on as a client if they have controversial opinions," Emerson went on. "She said you only like to play it safe."

Max didn't contradict her. "Yes, that's probably true."

"And Sarah has many controversial opinions," Emerson said. "It's not just the censorship thing, although I don't know how it's controversial that kids should have access to classics in the library. But she's also on board with teaching students that it wasn't just white men who made a difference in this country over the years."

Sarah didn't argue with that. She knew kids didn't learn enough about the contributions of women and minorities. She remembered seeing the movie and reading the book *Hidden Figures*, which told about the black women who were integral in the early space program. Behind the scenes, they were doing complex mathematical calculations for the astronauts and working in engineering at NASA. Their contributions were crucial to the early astronauts.

Yet Sarah had never even heard their stories until the book and the movie came out. In school, she studied about the white guys who went up in space, but nothing about the black women who helped them get there. And that was just one example out of many. Sarah wanted to encourage the school to require one class that focused on the contributions of women and nonwhites to the nation's history. She didn't think that should be a controversial requirement.

But, apparently, it was. She couldn't imagine why it would be, but schools apparently thought it was appropriate to continue to pretend that only white males contributed to our nation's history. Well, maybe that was a slight exaggeration, but there was no doubt that dead white guys still dominated the conversation in our nation's schools, and Sarah found that appalling.

Sarah smiled at Max. "I'm not a radical. I'm just somebody who believes in equality and respect for everybody. And if you ask me if school studies need to be less white-male-centered, I'll say yes, definitely. It would be nice if the students knew more about Marie Curie, for instance, and her pioneering work on radioactivity. It would be great if the students would learn about the contributions of Barbara Strozzi, rather than just learning about Beethoven, Handel and Mozart."

Max gave her a strange look. "Barbara who?"

Sarah shook her head. "Exactly. Barbara Strozzi was a prolific composer during the Baroque Period. She composed music and was considered the most prolific composer of secular music during her time. Not the most prolific female composer, but the most prolific composer, period. And she did this even though she wasn't supported by the church or wealthy patrons, as musicians typically were back then."

Sarah smiled, even though she, herself, had never heard of Barbara Strozzi until Emerson schooled her on all the female composers that had lived. Turned out Emerson was a bit of an expert on the topic of female composers, not just because she was a very talented violinist who made a point of studying composers in general, but also because her feminist heart led her to really study the female ones.

Emerson had recently zeroed in on the goal of being a composer herself. She knew all the best composers were doing film scores and that almost all of them were men. She wanted to change that and blaze a trail for women to break through the male composer glass ceiling.

Emerson piped up. "Barbara Strozzi is just one female classical composer that people have never heard of. There are so many other ones. But nobody knows anything about them because the only composers anybody ever hears about are the white guys."

Max put his hands up. "I can see I'm being double-teamed here," he said. "By two card-carrying feminists."

Emerson rolled her eyes. "You call us card-carrying feminists. I call us two bad bitches tired of white dudes always getting all the glory. And kids must realize that women and nonwhite people have made contributions. Important ones. It sucks that nobody knows about Pauline Viardot, Ethel Smyth, or Francesca Caccini. Or that women wrote operas at all."

Emerson was referring to three women who were among many that wrote operas.

"Everybody knows about that Shakespeare dude, but nobody knows about Aphra Behn." Emerson was talking about the female playwright who lived in the late 17th century. "Or about any female playwrights. We study Tennessee Williams, Arthur Miller and William Inge, but nobody knows about Lillian Hellman and Marsha Norman." Lillian Hellman and Marsha Norman were two living playwrights who penned such classics as *The Children's Hour* and *'Night Mother,* which won the Pulitzer Prize for Drama in 1983. Marsha Norman also adapted the books *The Color Purple, The Secret Garden* and *The Bridges of Madison County* for the Broadway stage.

Sarah shrugged her shoulders at Max and gave him an apologetic look. Like most people, he was clearly unaware of many female and nonwhite contributors to history and the arts. But that didn't mean he was an ignorant cretin, as he apparently was feeling like. It was clear by the look on his face he was embarrassed by his lack of knowledge and that he was being schooled by a 13-year-old girl.

She knew how he felt. She, herself, was being schooled by the same 13-year-old girl. And she knew that Max came from her generation. Generation X, the generation that both she and Max belonged to, wasn't as aware as Emerson's generation about how unequal education was. She didn't know a single trans person in high school or junior high. She never thought too much about the fact that the lessons taught in school gave short shrift, which was an understatement, to people who weren't white men. She took German history and barely learned about the Holocaust. She was taught nothing about slavery or indigenous people in her American history class.

There was just so much their generation wasn't exposed to. And, looking back, Sarah thought that was wrong. But it wasn't until Emerson came along that Sarah realized how wrong it was and how things needed to change. Now, apparently, Max was getting the same lessons she'd been getting. And he wasn't so thrilled about that prospect, judging by the look on his face.

"I see I have my work cut out for me," Max said with a smile.

"Damn straight," Emerson said with her hands on her hips. "And if you don't mind helping this bad bitch win a school board election, go for it. But know that I'll be on her butt the whole way. I'll push her to make the changes that need to be made at the school. So, you're getting a package deal."

"Noted," Max said.

"So, Emerson is much smarter than me," Sarah said.

"And much more informed. But she's right. All those changes she wants to see, I want to see. I think it's tragic that I'd never heard of those female playwrights or composers before, either. Or about nonwhite and female scientists, mathematicians and leaders. So, that'll also be part of my platform - changing the curriculum to make it more inclusive."

Max just nodded his head. "I agree with both of you about all that. But I still can't get on board with the censorship thing. I just think that there are books that our students shouldn't be exposed to. And you're not going to get me to move off that position."

Emerson cocked her head. "Is it about your daughter? About what happened to her?"

Max's face went very pale. "I don't want to talk about that."

Sarah looked over at Emerson, who had her hand over her mouth as if she realized she had said something wrong. "My bad. I shouldn't have gone there."

Sarah now knew that there was a story. Maybe this story would explain why Max was so weird about censorship. Sarah hoped not, because she had again changed her mind about her own position on censorship. Hallie had played a good Devil's advocate, which made Sarah question whether certain books should be in the library. But Emerson had convinced her that kids were exposed to much worse in their everyday life online. This made Sarah go back to her absolutist position that none of the books should be banned, either in the library or in the classroom.

Max cleared his throat. "Sarah, while I don't agree with your views on what books are appropriate for our young kids, I agree about everything else you've told me. And Emerson's right. I don't take controversial clients. Not anymore. I fear I've played it safe since I've been here on this island. And maybe it's time to shake things up just a little."

Emerson was quiet. It looked like she knew she'd gone too far when she brought up the subject of his daughter. Sarah was slightly amazed because she'd never known Emerson to back down on any topic. Yet it seemed she was going to step back just a little from the conversation.

It seemed like such an odd reaction from Emerson. Sarah got to wondering exactly what the young girl was talking about.

Max stayed for three hours, guiding Sarah through the process of filing her paperwork, finding volunteers, funding her campaign, and planning events. He was a great help to her, and by the time he left that evening, Sarah was feeling much more confident about her campaign.

But she knew she was going to have to talk to Emerson. She wanted to find out what the young girl knew about Max and why she asked him if he was hesitant to help Sarah because of his daughter.

So, after Max left, Sarah talked to Emerson while the two did the dishes from the dinner. "What's going on?" she asked Emerson.

Emerson shrugged her shoulders. "I don't know what you're talking about."

"I think you do. I think you know something about Max. Not that it's any of my business, except it might affect his beliefs about the whole censorship thing."

Emerson just looked at Sarah and gave Sarah a look that said that Sarah wasn't going to get anything out of her.

"Sarah, I might have a big mouth. And sometimes, I don't know when to keep my mouth shut. So, just forget I said anything about Max's daughter. Because it's not my business."

Well, that was weird. Emerson, admitting that she had a big mouth? And, even odder, she was self-conscious about that fact and wanted to take back something she said. Sarah definitely wasn't used to Emerson being so self-reflective. And that was one of the things that Sarah loved about the girl. Like Sarah's own mother, Emerson usually didn't have a filter.

"Okay. I guess you have some kind of loyalty to somebody?"

Emerson nodded her head. "Julia. She told me some stuff that I'm not supposed to talk about. I know it sucks when you bring something up and then say you can't talk about it. That's the worst. Why bring it up if you're not going to discuss it? But, in this case, I opened my mouth before thinking. So just pretend I never said anything."

Sarah didn't want to admit it, but she was curious about what Emerson hid from her. And she hated that it probably wasn't something that concerned her. Yet, it was going to bother her that she had no idea what was not being said.

"Okay. You don't have to say anything. I'm not going to force it out of you."

"Thanks." Emerson finished rinsing off a dish and put it into the dishwasher. "I think I've changed my mind about Max. Dude's legit. I think he might really be able to help you."

Sarah raised an eyebrow. "Oh, you do, do you? You sure were convinced he was out to sabotage me. Why did you think that?"

Emerson shrugged her shoulders. "I don't know why I

thought that. I just got the impression from Julia that Max was much weirder about the censorship thing than he really was. But he's not weird about it. So, I think you guys might actually make a great team."

Sarah smiled. "So, I have your blessing, then?"

"Yeah. Plus, have you noticed he has a cute butt?" Then she raised her eyebrows and laughed.

Sarah cocked her head. "No, I honestly never noticed his butt." She wanted to tell Emerson that while she never noticed Max's posterior, she did notice his beautiful green eyes and dimples. She always did crush on a young Tom Hanks.

"He must do a lot of squats," Emerson said with another raise of her eyebrows.

"Yeah, he must," Sarah said with a laugh.

But Sarah felt a bit uncomfortable about discussing Max's physical attributes because she realized he was an attractive guy. And Sarah, having gotten out of a long, toxic relationship with a billionaire who wanted to control her, vowed not to get involved with another man. Not just for a while, but forever.

And she didn't like being attracted to a guy.

Let alone to a guy that she was going to be regularly seeing.

Chapter Fourteen

Ava

After Ava had dinner with Chris and Samantha at her house, she started to believe that maybe, just maybe, she and Chris could become friends again. That was all she really imagined the relationship would become. She still didn't trust him. She still didn't know where that money came from that he had paid her, so she refused to touch even a dollar of that money. Not that Chris was ever involved in criminality, but he borrowed millions of dollars from Chinese loan sharks. She never imagined that he would do something like that, either. So, she imagined that Chris was capable of more than Ava had ever thought he would be.

In the meantime, Ava decided she would go ahead and call Chris's sister. He'd given Ava his sister Nicole's phone number because he knew Ava doubted his story about why it was he was really on the island. The old Ava, the Ava who was married to Chris, wouldn't have called Nicole to check up on his story. She was trusting of her husband. She had no reason not to be at that time.

But he had since given her reason not to trust him. To say the very least. So now Ava's motto regarding Christopher was that he would be guilty until proven innocent. And he might never be proven innocent again in her eyes.

So, Ava called Nicole, who was friendly enough to her. Ava had met her a time or two before, so it wasn't an entirely cold call.

"Hello, Ava," Nicole said to her in a friendly-enough voice. "How are you?"

"Fine. I just wanted to call you because Chris is on the island, and he told me the reason why he was on the island was that he was helping you."

"Helping me do what?" Nicole asked Ava.

Damn! Ava knew she couldn't trust Christopher. She cleared her throat. "Never mind. Christopher told me the story about you going through a divorce and staying with him at a hotel while he helps you sort things out."

She started to laugh. "I'm not married. And where are you living?"

"Nantucket."

"I'm living across the country. In San Diego." And then she paused. "How odd. Well, my brother has always been one to make up stories. But no, I'm not going through a divorce, mainly because I've never been married. But tell him I say hello. I haven't talked to him in a year or more."

Ava got off the phone and immediately called Chris. "Hey," Ava said to Chris after he picked up. "You lied to me."

Chris said nothing for about a minute. The dead air hung between Ava and Chris as Ava impatiently waited for him to address her accusation.

Finally, he spoke. "You talked to Nicole." That was not a question but a defeated statement.

"Damn straight. Now I'm starting to wonder if anything you told me the other night was true." Ava kicked herself when she thought about the questions she could've asked Nicole. Not that she would've asked intrusive questions about their father's suicide and about whether or not said father actually molested her. Ava had to think that story was true because who would make up something like that?

"Ava, I can explain."

"Nope. Two strikes and you're out."

"That's not the right saying. It's usually three strikes and you're out."

"Chris, the first strike, your stealing from me, was so gigantic it should count as two strikes. So, technically, this would be your third strike. And you're out."

Chris let out a heavy sigh. "Ava, I'm so sorry lied to you about Nicole."

"You not only lied to me. But you took me for a fool. A damned fool. You probably gave me her phone number because you thought I wouldn't call her. I imagine you thought that if you gave me her phone number, surely that would be enough for me to know you were telling the truth. The old reverse psychology trick. Well, newsflash. That kind of nonsense doesn't work on me."

"You're right. I never should've imagined that you would've been dumb enough to fall for that. After all, you were a lawyer. And I know that, as a lawyer, you're going to go by facts and evidence. You want provables."

Ava just shook her head. What was up with Chris? She never knew him to be somebody who would be so clumsy about lying. For that matter, during their marriage, she didn't think he was one to be a liar anyhow. Now, here he was, throwing out a lie and then daring her to find out the truth.

And then acting so surprised when she actually did find out the truth.

What a tool.

"Ava, I'm on your porch right now. I really want to talk to you."

Ava just shook her head. She was in the sunroom, which was on the second floor. It was attached to the outdoor terrace that she loved so much. And, usually, she would be on that terrace. But today, it was unusually cold out. And, suddenly, Ava felt even colder.

"Chris, turn around and leave. You're not welcome in this house."

To her dismay, however, she heard Chris coming up the stairs. She knew it wasn't Jessica, because she knew Chris's step cadence. That's how well she knew him – just like a mother animal could hear her baby's cries, even if there were a flock of other animals also crying, Ava could distinguish Chris's steps from anybody else's.

So, she didn't even bother to turn around when she heard Chris coming into the room. "Chris, I'm serious about what I said. I don't know why you're here. And how did you get in here, anyhow?"

"Jessica let me in." Chris's voice sounded heavy, as if he was trying to hold back tears.

"I'll have to have a talk with Jessica later about that. But, for now, I'd like you to show yourself out. And never come back."

"Ava, I made up the story about my sister. I panicked. I didn't know what to tell you about why I was on this island. I've been trying so hard to come up with a story to tell you, but the truth is I'm on this island just for you."

Ava finally spun around in her chair. "Oh, no. No. You're not going to tell me that. Because I'm going to tell you that if there's nothing holding you here, you probably should get on with your life somewhere else. Because the longer you're on this island, the more you're getting away from what you need to do to get your life together. Getting a job. Staying away from the gambling tables. Maybe finding another woman who's going to put up with your BS."

Ava regretted that last recommendation. Because she believed in her heart that Chris was no good for anybody. She didn't used to believe that there were people in the world who didn't belong with somebody. She used to think there was a lid for every pot - everybody in the world was meant for somebody. She no longer believed that. She now thought that some people were just so dysfunctional, so damaged, they would ruin the life of anybody unlucky enough to share their life with that person.

In other words, there were just people in the world who were undateable. People like Lauren, Sarah's former friend and current nemesis, were undateable. Lauren was such a garbage person that she threw Sarah under the bus and left Sarah to take the blame for her own drugs. This was after Sarah came out in the middle of the night to drive her home when Lauren was too wasted to get behind the wheel herself.

A person like Lauren who would do that to another person was someone Ava considered a person who should be alone in her life forever. Because nobody deserved the kind of treatment that a narcissistic sociopath like Lauren was bound to dish out.

Of course, Lauren probably wasn't alone in life. She probably was tormenting somebody right now with her narcissistic amoral self.

Ava didn't even believe, as some people believed, that a garbage person deserved to be with another garbage person. Let two terrible people get together. That way, they can torment each other instead of tormenting an innocent person, goes the theory. But Ava didn't believe that, either. Two garbage people together would only consolidate their overall crazy and become more powerful that way. And God forbid there were any children involved.

To Ava, if truly garbage people would just recognize they weren't suitable for anybody, many of the world's problems would be resolved. There would be no children witnessing abusive situations; no women making excuses for their disgusting, womanizing husbands; no men being taken advantage of by their grasping and greedy wives. Therapists would go out of business if crazy people would just isolate their crazy and not try to subject another person to them.

Now Ava was thinking that Chris belonged in the undateable category. Because she didn't think that anybody should be subjected to his lies and evident narcissism.

"Ava, please just hear me out. I made such a mistake when I did what I did to you. I found out you were living here and wanted to be close to you. But I knew I couldn't be close to you because I couldn't devise a good enough excuse for why I would want to live here. So, I came up with the sister thing. It was lame, I admit. But it was the only thing I could think of."

Ava rolled her eyes. "And what would've happened if you just would've told me the truth - assuming that what you're telling me now is the truth? It's not like I could've voted you off the island like on *Survivor*. Although, if I had the power to do that, I would've."

"That's exactly why. I couldn't have ever convinced you to give me a chance if you thought I was just hanging around this island for no reason. But it would've been different if I had a reason to be here. I would've had an excuse to hang around, and then we could have slowly gotten to know each other again."

Ava shook her head. If Christopher was telling her the truth, then it was pathetic. Flattering, but pathetic. But Ava wasn't sure he was even telling her the truth now. What if he was on the island for a much more nefarious reason? Maybe he was in touch with a drug dealer on the island who had a big yacht and was a soldier for the kingpin. Maybe the kingpin was the person who bankrolled his gambling addiction, and now Chris owed him.

Ava knew her imagination was running amok, and there was no stopping it. Besides, his silly story didn't ring true to her. What, he didn't think she would check up on the sister thing? She didn't think he was so bad of a chess player that he wouldn't have seen just a few moves ahead.

Ava bit her bottom lip. She was going to have to make a trip to Willow's spa. The psychic would be able to tell her if Chris was on the level or not.

Because one thing was for sure. Her radar, at least where Chris was concerned, was damaged. She didn't necessarily like visiting Willow to ask her for answers, but she didn't feel she had a choice.

"Chris, let me get one thing straight with you. There's no chance here. You and me, that's never going to happen. And when I say never, I mean never. Ever. You can stay on his island for 100 years, but it ain't happening."

Chris just nodded his head. He seemed so defeated still in his life that Ava almost felt sorry for him. He was never like that when he was married to her. After all, he was an investment banker - hard-charging, hard-working and involved in high-stress, high-risk deals. He was a mover and a shaker. He was not this defeatist person who was standing in front of her. He always had a ton of energy, sometimes too much. But, as he stood in front of her, his shoulders slumped, and his eyes cast down, he looked like nothing but a sad sack.

Ava shook her head. *What changed you, Christopher?* Perhaps his story about his family was true, and his father really did commit suicide after having molested his sister. But there was something more. There was something that made him go off the deep end.

Somehow, Ava didn't believe that having a parent commit suicide, a parent you weren't close with, would be enough to take somebody from a confident, successful banker who hobnobbed with wealthy people to losing millions at the poker table and hitting rock bottom.

Ava raised an eyebrow. He still was standing in front of her, even though he was never invited on the premises in the first place. In fact, she told him to leave before he ever came in the door. As of now, he was only a trespasser. She could call the cops to get rid of him, but she thought that was excessive.

He finally just nodded his head. "Okay. I'll leave."

And then he quietly went down the stairs. Ava heard him at the bottom of the stairs, talking to Jessica. Ava closed her eyes because she knew Jessica would be coming to talk to her soon.

Of course, she was right about that.

"Ava," Jessica said as gently as possible. "Chris just left. He told me you wanted nothing to do with him."

"No lie detected," Ava said.

"It's not my business. But I think Chris is fragile. I worry about him."

Ava took a deep breath. "Jessica. I know you know

things about him because he's in your AA group. But I don't know those same things about him. And even the things he tells me, I don't think I can trust. So, unless you're willing to tell me exactly what you know about him, your first instinct was correct. It's not your business."

Jessica's face flushed red, and Ava momentarily regretted her harsh words with her young friend. She had never been harsh with Jessica before. She'd never spoken to her in a less than friendly tone. And it was clear that Jessica's heart was in the right place.

But even if Jessica's heart was in the right place, she was overstepping her bounds. Ava wanted her just to mind her business and stay out of her relationship with Christopher.

Jessica just nodded her head. "I'm sorry, Ava. I didn't mean to step on your toes. It's just that when I see somebody who's in pain, I just want to soothe them. I see many people in psychic pain in my meetings, and I want to hug every last one of them and try to take their troubles away. And I think that Chris is troubled more than most. He's really lost a lot."

"Yeah, he's lost a lot. He lost millions of dollars."

"I'm not talking about money." And then Jessica opened her mouth as if she was going to say something else but obviously thought better of it because she immediately closed her mouth again. "Never mind."

Ava put her hand on Jessica's shoulder to show Jessica she wasn't angry with her. "Listen, Jessica. I know you're in a tough spot. You're required by the ethics of your AA meeting not to disclose confidential information you learn in the meetings. I understand that, and I respect it. And I know you want to tell me what you know about Christopher. You think that maybe it'll change my mind about him. But I don't think there's anything that'll change my mind about him. But I'll tell you what I'll do. Since I'm not getting a straight answer from him, and you can't tell me straight answers, I'm going to see Willow. Maybe she can tell me something about what I'm missing here."

Jessica smiled and nodded her head. "That's a good idea. Willow is really psychic. Maybe she can give you answers."

Ava hoped so. But she knew that even Willow wasn't perfect with her psychic readings. She was good. Very good. But sometimes, it seemed that she only got half the information she needed. So Ava thought she might get some answers, but probably not all of them.

But some answers were better than nothing.

Chapter Fifteen

Ava

Ava went to the spa co-owned by her best friend Hallie and Willow Killeen, a young psychic and tarot reader who also happened to be proficient with acupuncture, herbal therapy, sound therapy, and aromatherapy. If there was a metaphysical way of healing, Willow was an expert at it.

Willow even helped Hallie recover from cancer. Of course, Hallie went through chemotherapy and had surgery to remove the tumor in her breast. But she had a lot of ill effects from the chemo, such as nausea and weakness. Willow helped Hallie get over the sickness she felt from the chemotherapy by combining acupuncture and chakra therapy.

While Willow never called herself a witch, sometimes Ava thought that some practices sounded a bit like the Wicca practices that Ava had heard about. For instance, Willow practiced rituals that involved her summoning goddesses and gods in helping with healing practices. Ava couldn't judge Willow for that because if it helped, that was all that mattered.

And now Ava was going to ask Willow to help her by using her special powers. A year ago, she would've felt silly going to a psychic for anything. But she had seen, time and again, Willow perform her magic, so there was just no denying it. Willow was the real deal.

She walked into the spa, and a little bell clinked. Willow was working behind the computer, and she was not accompanied by Hallie. Usually, Hallie was hanging around the spa. But she wasn't on that day.

Willow nodded her head. "Ava. What's new?"

Ava took a breath. And, to her surprise and shock, she burst into tears. She had no idea why she was crying. She certainly didn't plan to cry in front of Willow, not that Willow would've judged her.

Willow came over to her and wrapped her arms around her. "Ava, what is it?"

Ava sniffled and shook her head. "I don't know. I have no idea why I'm crying. Maybe I have more feelings for my ex-husband than I've acknowledged. And, if so, that's disastrous. Just disastrous."

Willow hugged her tight. "And you're here to see me because you want answers." And then Willow closed her eyes. "I've got nothing on this guy. I'm sorry. He has a kind of a protective veil around him. That sometimes happens with people. I can usually get a read on anybody, except folks with an emotional block. And I think that guy you're talking about has that kind of a block. But, I can throw some cards out for you if you like."

Ava just nodded her head and said nothing. She didn't want to start bawling again, and she thought that if she opened her mouth, nothing would come out but a primal scream.

Ava followed Willow into the back room, where the young psychic did her tarot readings. She felt nervous, but she knew she shouldn't. Willow was going to reveal something, although Ava had no idea what that something was. But Ava shouldn't care either way. Should she?

As Willow shuffled the cards, she asked Ava a few questions. "Now, tell me what happened."

Ava told her everything about Chris just showing up out of the blue. She told Willow all about how he left her and stole from her. She also told her about how Jessica seemed to want her to give Chris a chance. And then she told her about Chris lying about why he was on the island.

She'd hoped Willow would just have the answer for her. That Willow could just tell her everything that was on Chris's mind. But, no. Chris was such an inscrutable guy that even Willow couldn't read his mind. And that was saying something.

Willow cut the cards and asked Ava which half of the deck she wanted Willow to work with. Ava tapped the one on the left, and Willow threw out the cards.

Willow arranged them into a pattern. "It's called the Celtic Cross," Willow said as she carefully put the cards into one line of three cards, with a fourth card laid over the second one, two cards on either side of the three-card line, and then another line of four cards on the outside of the pattern.

Willow studied the cards. "It looks like he left in a hurry, without any warning. You can see The Tower in the past and The Devil in the environment part of the reading. But things seem to be getting better. The Six of Swords in the present indicates that whatever made him want to leave might be in the past, and he's moved into calmer waters in his life."

Ava nodded her head, absorbing all that Willow was giving to her in bits and pieces.

"What else is in these cards?" she asked Willow.

"Well, there's definitely a child in the mix who was an obstacle. The princess of cups. A tender, sensitive child. Since her card was crossing his, that was part of why he left. But the card representing him is very positive - Ace of Cups. He loved this child with all his heart, but she caused him great pain."

Ava froze when Willow told her about the child thing. That confused her. Chris had no children of his own. Maybe that princess of cups was one of her children - probably Samantha. She was tender and sensitive.

But why would Samantha have anything to do with Chris's leaving? That didn't make a lick of sense.

Willow went on with the reading. "See, I think Chris is a very fragile person. And I just see a kind of breakdown with him, like he just couldn't face up to life. Three of Swords in the subconscious slot shows a great deal of sorrow but combined with The Devil and The Tower shows a mental breakdown of some sort. A secret addiction shows up in the reading like he was dealing with some kind of drug, alcohol, or gambling problem that he kept hidden from the world."

That rang true, of course. Willow was seeing his gambling addiction. But Chris, fragile? No.

Yes. Chris *was* fragile now. Ava sensed it, and Jessica confirmed it. But why was he? So many questions.

"What else do you see?" Ava asked.

"Well, he seems to fear you. Not just you, but all the

people he loves. You can see Two of Cups here in the fears section. That card represents love, and he's deathly afraid of it for some reason. Yet he longs for the people he loves because this section also represents his hopes."

Ava closed her eyes. This reading wasn't turning out the way she imagined it would. She was hoping Willow would tell her something to seal her hatred for Chris. Instead, Willow was making Ava sympathetic to him again.

"What's the outcome?" Ava asked her.

"The Sun. It's a very positive card. It's the brightness coming after a very dark time. See, in this spread, I see so much darkness all through it, but the sun comes out in the end."

Ava had mixed feelings about the Sun card coming out at the end. She wondered what it meant. "What do you suppose that Sun card means in this context?"

Willow shook her head. "It's a very positive card, but it might just mean that Chris finally finds some happiness in his life. I don't think it means you guys will get back together if that's what you're thinking." And then Willow cocked her head. "You're worried. You think maybe he's involved in something illegal, and that's why he's here on the island. I can feel your vibrations. It's really strong."

"Is he involved in something illegal?"

Willow shook her head. "No. There's no sign he's involved in something illegal. But he was, at one time. I think he got sucked in with some bad people, and –" She stopped. "He almost died. I'm not sure about the circumstances. I just am getting that he had a near-death experience, and that's why he's here."

Ava's ears perked up. Finally, something was making sense. "Go on."

Willow closed her eyes like she was concentrating hard. But then she shook her head. "I was starting to get a read, but then it just kind of vanished. Sorry. I guess we'll have to go with the card reading. This guy is really hard to read."

Ava pointed to the card that represented the small child. "I want to go back to that. Chris doesn't have any kids. I guess I'm just confused."

"There's something he's not telling you." She threw out another card. It was a picture of a beautiful woman with flowing hair staring contemplatively at a giant orb. "The moon. Deception. Sometimes it means illusions, but when paired with the seven of swords," she said, throwing out the seven of swords, "Deception is almost guaranteed."

Ava put her hand to her chin. "So, what kind of lie do you think he's telling me? Is it benign or more nefarious?"

Willow studied the spread she had laid out previously and then looked at the other two cards. "It's mixed. It's not something illegal, but it's quite underhanded. And I think it might be related to the princess of cups. Somehow I think that card is the center of it all. It's like the Rosetta Stone on this guy. If you can figure out what this card represents, you can unlock everything else with this guy."

Huh. All very peculiar. A small child and a near-death experience. Ava wondered if the two things were related and if they were all somehow interconnected with his visit to her.

"Is there anything else you can tell me?" Ava asked her.

"I'm not getting anything right now."

Ava paid her, even though Willow always insisted she did these tarot readings for her friends for free. But Ava, of course, wouldn't hear of her arguments. Willow had to eat, too, after all. "Thanks," she said to Willow. "You've given me a few things to chew on. A few things to ask Chris about, at any rate."

"Good luck. He's going to be a hard nut to crack."

That was an understatement, Ava thought.

The understatement of the year.

Chapter Sixteen

Sarah

Quinn informed Sarah that she had found a wealthy patron for Sarah's first fundraising venture. "Her name is Marilyn Williams. Her husband is a wealthy hedge fund manager, and she's another interior designer on the island. We've become good friends. I told her what you were doing, and she was really excited. She has a kid in the school and is on board with your positions. She has a 22-room house on Madaket, and she loves to give parties. She needs a good excuse to have a party, so she'd love to have a fundraiser for you."

Sarah was thrilled to hear the news. She wanted to do her campaign right, so she would invest in flyers, yard signs, and even employees if she couldn't find volunteers to knock on doors and phone bank. She felt she needed to do all these things because her name recognition wasn't very high on the island. She didn't know a lot of people on Nantucket. It wasn't that she didn't meet a lot of people, because she did, at Ava's B&B. But the people she met usually were transitory because they were staying at the inn and were usually on vacation.

But Quinn was meeting a lot of people through her job. So she was getting the connections on the island that Sarah would need to take advantage of if she had any chance of prevailing in her campaign. Hallie was also meeting people because she was a co-owner of a popular spa. So Hallie could also be a gold mine for making connections.

Sarah nervously called Max to tell him the news about the fundraiser.

"That's great!" Max said when Sarah called him. "Sounds like you're on your way."

"I am. Thanks to you."

"What did I do? I just came over and helped get your paperwork filed and gave you ideas about how to organize. You're the one who managed to get a fundraiser with a wealthy patron. And, trust me, you'll get some really nice dollars from this event."

"Maybe." Sarah bit her bottom lip. "Are you free? I mean, I could use a plus one."

Sarah closed her eyes, wondering what she was doing. Did she just ask this guy on a date? Yes, yes, she did.

"I happen to be free that evening," he said tentatively. "I mean, Julia has a sleepover Friday night. Otherwise, I'd have to beg off."

Sarah chuckled a little. "I'd love to have you there with me. You know, I need my campaign manager by my side when I meet these fancy donors. So, I'm glad you're going to be able to be there to support me."

"Yes. I do believe in you, you know. Even if you don't have the same views I do about censorship."

Sarah and Max talked on the phone for a few more

minutes, and Sarah hung up. She suddenly felt extremely nervous, and she had no idea why.

However, Emerson wasn't too happy about Sarah's tête-à-tête with Max that night. Or so Sarah found out when she had dinner at Quinn's house the Thursday before the fundraiser. Quinn told Sarah she would make her dinner because she'd been so good about watching Emerson. Ava and Hallie were also in attendance. That night's menu was vegetable lasagna, which was chock full of mushrooms, carrots, bell peppers, onions and zucchini. These vegetables were all garden fresh, as Quinn had taken up gardening in her spare time and was able to grow some beautiful things in her backyard garden.

After dinner, everybody gathered in Quinn's living room for wine and to talk about what would happen at the fundraiser. "It's not going to be a huge fundraiser," Quinn said. "Only around 50 people. But they're 50 wealthy people, so hopefully, it'll be a barnburner for you."

Emerson raised her eyebrow at Sarah. "You bringing Max to this thing?" she asked Sarah.

Sarah blushed a little bit and then took a sip of her wine. It was strange that she found this man so attractive. He was different from Nolan, but that was good for Sarah. Nolan was a billionaire who lived in a 20,000-square-foot mansion on a beautiful beach in Monterey, had a yacht and traveled the world with Sarah by his side. On the other hand, Max was a simple farmer who appeared to have a simple lifestyle. And he was the first man Sarah had felt attracted to since Nolan died.

"I am," Sarah said.

Emerson shook her head. "I knew it. I knew it. You got the hots for that dude."

"I do not," Sarah said. "He's my campaign advisor. He's

really helping out. It's the least I can do for him. I know that if I bring him to this fundraiser, he might be able to pick up another client for City Council or for the school board. Local government always needs some talented and dedicated people to make everything work. And he knows how to spot raw talent. So, I think him coming to this fundraiser with me is a win-win."

Hallie grinned. "Sarah, you're blushing. I think you do like this guy."

Ava thought the entire thing was so amusing. "Hallie's right. You're blushing. My sister, the girl who always had every man falling at her feet, is blushing about a guy. Who knew?"

"It's only professional," Sarah said, protesting everybody ganging up on her about this Max thing. "Really. I'm not interested in him except for what he can do for me on my campaign."

"I'm calling BS," Emerson said. "You know, I never thought you'd be so basic."

"I'm not basic," Sarah protested. "And I'm not hot for the campaign advisor."

But even as she said that she wondered if she really did have the hots for this guy.

As much as she didn't want to, she had to admit he made her feel tingly. And what was so wrong with that?

Chapter Seventeen

Ava

Ava knew after talking to Willow that she would have to confront Chris. She wasn't going to let him wriggle off the hook.

And she also knew she'd have to talk to him about the two of them formally divorcing. That was in the works, and if Ava ever hoped to move on with anybody else in her life, she needed to be legally free.

So, she invited him over to her house to talk. He was eager to see her, judging by his reaction to her invitation. "Ava, I was hoping you would come around. I knew you didn't hate me."

"I wouldn't go that far. And Chris, before you get any big ideas, one of the things I want to ask you about is making our marriage dissolution official. You're on the island, and so am I. I think it's time we finally do an equitable property division, get that piece of paper signed, and move on with it."

133

Chris got very quiet over the phone. "Ava, let's just slow things down a little when it comes to the divorce thing. We don't have to make it official just yet, do we?"

Ava couldn't believe what she was hearing. For over two years, she and Chris had been formally separated, if you could call it that. The only reason they weren't divorced was because Ava didn't know exactly where he was. Now that he was here on the island, Ava would take advantage of that.

"I don't know what you're talking about. We're hardly rushing into this. The marriage has been over for years. It was over long before you even left. And then when you left, it was really over. So this is a divorce that's been some seven years in the making. And I want to get on with it. I think we can come to an equal division of property."

Ava knew it was going to be just a bit complicated. After all, she had made hundreds of thousands of dollars off her bed and breakfast, and she would have to split that with Chris. And Chris probably had some profits he had made while they were separated. There would have to be an accounting of all that, which meant that both of them would have to get a good attorney to finalize everything. In reality, it was going to be a pain in the ass.

But Ava didn't want to think of that. It made her a little ill to think about how intrusive the entire division of property would be. Yet, it had to be done. Like a root canal, it was going to be a necessary evil.

"We'll talk about that," Chris said to Ava.

"Yes, we will."

So, that evening, Ava hosted Chris at her house. She made linguine with butter, garlic, and shrimp and served it with home-baked bread and her trusty bottle of wine.

Chris arrived that evening with another bottle of wine in his hand. He'd gotten a haircut and was wearing aftershave that he knew Ava liked. It was earthy, musky and spicy, with notes of Bergamot, Sandalwood and citrus.

As he stood there, his jet black hair cut close to his head, his big brown eyes with the long eyelashes looking at her with the expression he used to have for her when they were falling in love, Ava got a jolt. It was as if she saw how he looked 20 years ago when they met on the street. Ava was caught in the rain without an umbrella, and Chris, walking behind her on the busy Manhattan street, rushed up to her and shared his umbrella. Ava was grateful because she didn't want to go to her meeting looking like a drowned rat. So, when he insisted on walking with her to her office building, and she arrived at her office, she insisted on buying him a drink later that night.

Ava thought their relationship would be a good one because their story had such a meet-cute beginning and had started with such an act of chivalry. And it was. For a long time, it was.

Ava put her hands to her cheeks, and they felt warm.

He smiled. "I brought your favorite Pinot Grigio. I hope you don't tell me you're allergic to this, now, like with the oysters."

"God forbid I'd be allergic to wine," Ava said lightly. "I don't know what I would do with myself when wine o'clock rolls around."

She nodded her head at her husband. Chris always did know just what to bring her off the wine shelves. She liked her wines dry, for the most part, with just a hint of sweetness, and she liked them to be light-tasting. The Pinot Grigio Chris brought filled the bill on all fronts.

Ava brought out the dinner, and the two dug in with gusto. She was really hungry, and this particular pasta dish was her favorite. Chris also seemed to be enjoying the meal.

"Okay, Chris," Ava said after they finished their pasta and dessert, a chocolate raspberry layer cake Samantha had made for a fundraiser. She brought some home with her, which she shared with Ava. Ava was always amazed at how delicious Samantha's cakes were. Her daughter wasn't just talented with the design of the cakes but also with the baking part of it. No doubt about it, her daughter had found her niche. "We need to talk."

"I know. I'm sorry again about lying to you about why I was on the island."

"Don't worry about that. Listen, I think I know why you're here." She took a deep breath. "You almost died, and it made you appreciate life and realize that you didn't want to go meet your maker without settling things. The same thing happened with my mother. She watched the love of her life suddenly die and realized how short life was, so she vowed to make up with me. And she did. Now, I guess it's your turn."

Chris blinked. "How did you know about that?" he asked Ava.

"So, it's true? I was just trying to draw you out."

"Well, you're pretty good. But, you're right. I had an aneurysm. It was caused by a blood clot I got on a plane from Paris to Macau. I was lucky that the blood clot didn't kill me on the plane, and I ignored the headaches I got after landing. I was so focused on getting to the high-rolling tables that nothing would slow me down. Not a blood clot, and not the worst headache of my life."

Ava involuntarily put her hand to her chest and felt her heart beating. When Willow told her that Chris had a near-death experience, she assumed it was something like Chris had attempted suicide. After all, if Chris told her the truth about the bipolar thing, a suicide attempt would make sense. Suicide was always a risk when dealing with depression, which was one hallmark of the disease.

"So, what happened?"

"I had a mild stroke at the poker table. I was rushed to the hospital, and they found I had an aneurysm that had ruptured. I was lucky to come through surgery alive. And I know it. And that close call made me realize I was wasting my life."

Ava closed her eyes, imagining what Chris was going through. It had to have been difficult to be in a Chinese hospital for two weeks, although he knew the language at least. He was fluent in Mandarin Chinese because he learned it in his prep school growing up and studied it in college. He knew that China would be a huge client in his investment banking firm, so his ability to speak, read, and write in Mandarin was a huge asset to his firm.

"What was I doing?" Chris went on. "Sitting there, around strangers who didn't care about me. Losing money, hundreds of thousands of dollars a year. My life was a cesspool, and I sat in a hospital bed for two weeks. Two weeks, and of course, nobody visited me. I was in Macau. Who did I know there? I don't think I ever felt so alone in my entire life. And when you're sitting in a strange hospital bed in a foreign country, day after day, with nothing to do but think about where you went wrong in life, it makes you reevaluate everything. And when I got out of the hospital, I vowed I'd improve my life."

Ava cocked her head. She was getting a little bit past Chris's defenses. Peeling back the onion and seeing what was there. She felt his pain. It was palpable, and her heart went out to him.

"So, what happened after you got out of the hospital?"

Chris hesitated. "Well, I know you probably don't want

to hear this, but I thought of you a lot when I was in that hospital bed. I thought about the last time I was in the hospital. I broke my leg skiing. I know you remember that."

Oh, yes. Ava was never much of a skier. She could never see the appeal of participating in a sport where you're going to freeze your rear end off, get wet, and probably get hurt. Also, she was afraid of heights and had a recurring nightmare of getting stuck on the ski lift and being stuck there for hours or even overnight.

Ava's fear of the ski lift wasn't helped when she caught a movie on HBO called *Frozen* about three people stranded on a ski lift, two men and a woman. The two men jumped off the lift and got eaten by wolves, but they had to do something as they were all going to freeze to death otherwise. And, while that was only a movie, Ava had heard of people getting stuck on a ski lift and having to jump in real life.

But Christopher always liked to ski and had that in common with Jackson. Her son and husband were ski buddies on many trips to the Poconos, and Jackson also enjoyed snowboarding.

One trip went awry, however. Christopher fell down and broke his leg. He was in the hospital for two weeks that time, as well, and Ava was there at the hospital with him, by his side the whole time.

Ava nodded her head. "Yes, I do remember that skiing trip and that trip to the hospital. That's what you were thinking about when you were laid up in the hospital in Macau?"

"Yes. That's all I thought about. You were so good when I was in the hospital. You'd come over and sit on the uncomfortable chair next to the bed, and we played cards and board games and watched really bad movies together. Do you remember the day at the hospital we got sucked into an *America's Next Top Model* marathon? And we watched it for nine hours straight?"

Ava laughed as she thought of that day. She forgot exactly why they landed on that show, but Chris was right – the two of them couldn't stop watching it until they found out who won the crown of being America's Next Top Model. They got into all the competitions and the catfights, each choosing a favorite and somebody to hate. Ava's favorite was the one who won that year.

"Yeah. That actually was kind of a nice time. It was just you and me and a hospital bed. The kids were with a nanny that whole time. I was on vacation, and so were you, and we just didn't have any distractions. Aside from your broken leg, of course. But it was a time for us to just bond."

"Right. So, of course, I was getting a bit nostalgic as I lay there in the Macau hospital bed. I even tried to see if I could find *America's Next Top Model* on that TV because I wanted to re-create the Poconos hospital experience. I was very lonely and thought I had hit rock bottom. So, when I got out of the hospital, I was going to do anything I could to get the money back, so maybe you wouldn't hate me when I reappeared in your life. Hopefully, it worked."

"It did work, I guess. I mean, if you would've reappeared on the doorstep having not paid me back, I would've slammed the door in your face and called the police to get you gone. And then I would've gotten a restraining order. But I'm still very hesitant about that money. Where did you get it?"

Chris sighed. "I inherited the money from my dad. When he died, I became a multimillionaire. But I didn't want to touch that money for the longest time. I felt what he did to my sister was so dirty and wrong that I didn't want to touch a penny of that money. I realized I was being ridiculous about it because I was getting into debt with Chinese gangsters instead of accessing the money I was left by my father. I had to get therapy to understand that that money was mine, and it wasn't tainted or blood money. So I paid the gangsters back, and I paid you back. And then I paid Uncle Sam, and well, I'm broke. But happy. I don't know where my next dollar will come from, but I can look at myself in the mirror again."

Ava nodded her head. She hoped the explanation for the money was the truth, that he inherited the money from his father when his father committed suicide. After all, his father was extremely wealthy. If Chris could be believed about the origin of the money, then Ava felt she was safe to spend the money.

"Chris, I want to be fair to you. In all actuality, you were entitled to half the money you took. It was in a joint account that we contributed to over the years. I agree that you probably should have paid back at least half the money, plus a bit of interest, but you paid back the entire thing plus+50% interest, which was a bit excessive. So I guess I'm trying to say I can't keep all that money you gave me. I want to give you back at least half of it. That would only be right."

"Ava, no. I want you to keep all of it. I don't care I'm broke. I'm happy because I'm finally doing right by the people I hurt. I'm finally doing right by you. And I'm not completely broke. I have about $50,000 left. Enough to get me by until I find another job. And I still have mad investment banking skills, I was very good at my job, and my kind of experience is still very much in demand. Hopefully, I'll be working again in no time, making what I was making before, which means I won't be broke for long. So, please don't worry about me. I'll be fine."

Ava was a little bit uncomfortable with the whole situation. Chris was bending over backward to make up for what he did, but she didn't really want him to. She wanted to still be angry with him because she still didn't trust him, so it wasn't like she would get into another relationship with him. And because she didn't want another relationship with him, it was easier for her to continue to hate him.

But he was being so nice that it was difficult to continue despising him.

"Regardless, I'll give you half the money back you gave me. I have my respect and pride, and I don't feel entitled to all that money, and I don't want it."

Chris opened his mouth to argue, but Ava put her hand on his shoulder and squeezed. That was one of the things she had done before when they were married, and she wanted to make her point. Chris immediately recognized the move, and his body language showed he was acquiescing.

"Okay. If you want to give me half the money back, I guess I'll be forced to accept it. But I really want you to have it. It's the least I could do to make up for what I did to you."

Ava took a deep breath and sat back in her chair. "Thank you. I'll transfer the money tonight. You just have to give me your PayPal or Venmo information, and I'll figure out if I can transfer all that money to you at once or if I have to do it in increments. Probably the latter. I don't imagine PayPal or Venmo allows for such a large transfer."

Ava did a quick check and realized she was correct – Venmo definitely did not allow for such a large transfer. Ava was going to have to transfer through an ACH.

"I'll go to my bank today and I'll transfer that money to your account. No arguments."

Chris just nodded his head and took a deep breath.

"Ava, I don't know if it's too late for us. But I wanted to tell you that, whatever happens, I never stopped loving you. I don't know how to make up for everything I've done to you. And I've been really thinking about all I've done during our marriage, and I'm not proud of any of it."

Ava felt her heart thaw just a little. It was like a frozen pipe left out in the sun. But she didn't want that. She wanted to go on despising him. "Chris, what's done is done. You made good on the money. And you explained yourself. Now, if you could just tell me the rest, maybe we can move forward."

Chris looked at Ava with downcast eyes. That told Ava all she needed to know. "You're so sure there is more to the story?"

"Yes. And the reason why I believe that is because you told me before you ever told me anything about where you've been that I would hate you once I got the story. And all that implies that there's more." And then Ava furrowed her brows. "And there's some young girl involved in all this."

Ava threw that out there to see if he took the bait. And, he did. His face flushed bright red, and then his expression changed from nervous to terrified. Suddenly, Ava knew she was getting closer to the Rosetta Stone, just like Willow said.

Christopher took a deep breath. "Ava, I can't talk about this right now."

Ava sat back in her chair. "Chris, you have to talk about it. If only because we need to finally clear the air between us. Once and for all, I want the whole story. No more lies. No more omissions."

Chris finally looked defeated. "Okay. I'll tell you everything."

Chapter Eighteen

Sarah

That Friday evening, Sarah was a guest of honor at Marilyn Williams's fundraiser. She had met Marilyn earlier that day when she had lunch with her on Liam Williams's yacht. Liam Williams was a hedge fund manager who made billions of dollars a year, and the yacht he owned was called "Endless Summer." The yacht was 100 feet long and was all luxury. It was currently docked in the Nantucket Marina, part of the harbor.

That Friday afternoon, Sarah went to the yacht to meet Marilyn. Marilyn was 60 years old but apparently didn't let Father Time have his say. She had long jet black hair with blue streaks that were randomly highlighted throughout her hair, big green eyes with lush eyelash extensions, and permanent eyeliner. Her 5'7", 120-pound muscular frame was dressed in leather pants and a silk floral top, paired with Dior spiked black heels. She looked like she had never eaten a carb in her life. Sarah knew

Marilyn had come by her trim and muscular body the old-fashioned way – lots of weight training, cardio, and disciplined eating. The lady had discipline and probably a personal trainer or two.

Marilyn saw Sarah approaching the yacht, and she waved excitedly. "Sarah!" she said with a gleeful smile on her face. "Up here!"

Sarah boarded the yacht, and Marilyn hugged her as if Sarah was a long-lost friend. In reality, Sarah had never met the woman, but she liked her instantly. Marilyn just had that infectious, free-spirited vibe that Sarah was very drawn to.

"Sit, sit," Marilyn said, pointing to a table and chairs on the enormous yacht's deck. "I've got a dirty martini with your name on it. I hope you like lots of olive juice because I make my martinis filthy."

"I love olive juice, actually," Sarah said. "The more, the better." Sarah didn't care for martinis, in general, because she didn't like the taste of either vodka or gin, but she did like dirty martinis because the olive juice tended to cut the bite of the alcohol.

"I knew you'd be a kindred spirit," Marilyn said with a wink. "Quinn told me all about you, and I couldn't be more excited about meeting you. Your positions track all mine. I wish I could run to school board myself, but I'm not going to, so I'll have to live vicariously through you."

"Thank you so much for having this fundraiser for me," Sarah said. "On such short notice."

Marilyn waved her hand dismissively. "Oh, please. It's not a big deal. I like having parties. Any excuse to have a gathering, I'm there. I'm a party girl from way back. I was in a band back in the day. The Blue Unicorns. We're on Apple music if you want to take a listen sometime."

Sarah had no trouble imagining this woman fronting a

band. She seemed like the type that probably still played gigs on Saturday nights.

"You were in a band? Did you play an instrument, or did you sing?"

"Both. I played lead guitar, and I was also the lead singer. You should take a listen to our songs on Apple Music. You might be surprised. Anyhow, I wanted to meet with you and let you know what kind of a soirée we'll have tonight. It's going to be the usual - live band, open bar, buffet, and silent auction. And me, going around and glad-handing everybody. I'm the best ass-kisser you're ever gonna meet in your life. And trust me, you gotta be a world-class ass-kisser if you're going to succeed in raising money."

A guy brought lobster tails and a baked potato over to the table. Marilyn motioned to the waiter to bring them two more dirty martinis. And then she started speaking rapid Spanish to the guy. Sarah, of course, understood every word because she was very fluent in the language. Marilyn was talking to the guy about her, Sarah, telling him that Sarah was the one who was going to set the school right. Not that the waiter cared because it was obvious from his face – he had on a plastic smile – he couldn't care less. But Marilyn was effusive in her praise of her new friend, anyhow.

Sarah wondered if Marilyn was just blowing smoke up her ass. After all, Marilyn was telling Sarah how she was the best ass-kisser in the business. But she didn't think Marilyn was being insincere because Marilyn really seemed to believe in Sarah.

Marilyn turned back around. "Dig in. The lobster's fresh, caught just this morning, so the poor thing wasn't on death row for too long. I don't know. I hate seeing those poor creatures on top of each other in a tank, knowing their fate is they're going to soon be served with a butter sauce.

Anyhow, I can't think about that too much because I do love me some lobster tails."

Marilyn and Sarah dug into the tails, which were tender and flavorful and served with a butter sauce. Sarah was starting to get slightly buzzed off the two martinis.

"So, why did you decide to become a patron for me?" Sarah asked Marilyn.

"Because I think we're kindred spirits. I agree with you that one of your big platforms is no censorship. But mainly, I think our kids need to be taught the real history of this country. They also need to learn about novelists, musicians, poets, and artists who don't look like some pale white dude like my husband. Not that my husband is so bad-looking, but, damn, he's whiter than a ghost."

Sarah smiled as she realized she was on the same page as this woman. "Of course, I agree."

"Yeah. And I think our kids don't learn enough about persecution. Groups have always been persecuted worldwide, and it's just scapegoating. You know, your life's in the toilet because somebody else is taking what's rightfully yours. Tale as old as time. If kids could just learn a bit more about why scapegoating is so wrong, and who really is responsible for society's ills, maybe they can stop carrying on the prejudices of their parents and grandparents."

Sarah was curious about who Marilyn thought was responsible for society's ills. "I totally agree with what you're saying. Who do you think is responsible for what ails our country?"

"Don't even get me started," she said, shaking her head. "Trust me, I have my ideas about it, ideas my husband wouldn't be happy to listen to. At any rate, I think our kids should have more lessons about how different and various people have succeeded, and fewer lessons about us versus them."

When Sarah finally left the yacht, she counted Marilyn as a new friend. She invited her to one of the wine nights with Sarah and the ladies, and Marilyn eagerly accepted. "I'm always looking for a new girl group to hang out with, and it sounds like you and your ladies might fit the bill. Anyhow, I'll see you tonight. Just come on over. You don't have to get dressed up in some crazy formal gown. Just come as you are. I'll be doing the same. And, who knows, I might just get up and jam with the band. I do that from time to time."

So, that evening, Sarah went to the enormous house owned by Marilyn and her husband, Liam. Liam wasn't around because he apparently was on a business trip. There were a couple hundred people, most of them dressed casually, although a few of the men were in suit and tie, and some of the ladies were dressed in dresses. But, for the most part, the people were dressed in jeans and khakis.

Sarah, herself, was dressed in a sundress and espadrilles. She didn't want to go too casual because she was the guest of honor. She was arriving with Max by her side. He was dressed business casual in khakis, a button-down, and a light jacket.

Sarah didn't want to admit how much she thought Max looked adorable that night. He had just gotten a haircut, so his naturally curly hair was shorn very short on the sides, but the top was still curly. His green eyes had a playful twinkle and his dimples were distracting. She felt her heart start racing when he came to her door to pick her up for the fundraiser.

"I have to say, you managed one helluva feat in getting Marilyn Williams to host this thing. Most people running for the school board have to settle for some function in a church basement with sub sandwiches, cookies, and punch. And, if they're really lucky, the punch would be spiked."

"Well, my good friend Quinn is an interior decorator, and she knows many of the bigwigs here on the island. Marilyn's a lot of fun, so I'm really looking forward to this."

They got there, and the party was in full swing. Waiters were bringing around different hors d'oeuvres, and Sarah was starving, even though she had a nice lunch with Marilyn that day. Sarah eagerly took a glass of champagne from one waiter and a lobster puff from another.

Marilyn found her and waved to her from across the room. "Sarah, I want you to meet somebody. His name is-"

Sara smiled. "Langdon Prescott," she said. "We've met."

Langdon smiled at Sarah with a shy smile. Langdon and Sarah had met when Sarah was new on the island, and she was waiting tables. Langdon was having dinner with her former friend and current nemesis, Lauren. At one time, Sarah considered Lauren to be a frenemy. That was when they were hanging out, but Sarah knew Lauren was a vile creature. But after Lauren hung Sarah out to dry for her own drug possession, Lauren ceased being any kind of a friend to Sarah.

Sarah had since run into Langdon, and he flirted with her and asked her out. She had no interest in him, mainly because Lauren told Langdon that Sarah was a world traveler when she waited on him and Lauren. He asked Lauren in a snide voice how Sarah would have the money to go around the world. Because, after all, Sarah was only a waitress.

Now Sarah was not quite on her rear end like she was before. And she still had no interest in Langdon. To Sarah, Langdon was a rich preppy bastard who looked down on service people. Sarah had no patience for that kind of attitude.

Marilyn looked at Langdon and then at Sarah. "You guys met, great!" Then she nudged Sarah. "He's been bugging me about introducing you to him since you came in the door, so I'm surprised you guys know each other."

Langdon smiled. "I'm sure I'm not the only guy who's jonesing to meet you. But I'm really happy you remembered me. I didn't think you would."

"Of course, I remember you. You did me a solid when you gave me the address for Lauren's husband. I'm now not a convicted felon anymore, and that was because Lauren's husband came clean about what she did to me. So, I can thank you for that. And that's what I'm going to do right now - thank you."

And that was true. Langdon told Sarah about Lauren and her husband divorcing and that they had a house on Nantucket they would sell. So Sarah went to Lauren's Nantucket home, talked to her husband, and got what she was desperate for – a full confession on what Lauren and her husband did to Sarah. The husband came clean on all the bribery and influence he had exerted to ensure Sarah was convicted for Lauren's drugs.

More importantly, Lauren's husband wrote the governor of California about what he did. Sarah was able to get a full pardon mainly because of that confession. So, in a way, Sarah really did owe Langdon.

Langdon nodded his head. "How did all that shake out?" he asked.

"William wrote the governor of California, admitting what he did. So, it did the trick. I'm no longer a convicted felon."

When Sarah said that, Max, who was standing next to Sarah, looked at her with surprise. "What's that supposed to mean?"

Sarah took a deep breath. "Long story," she said with a roll of her eyes. "Very long story. I'll just say I not only got dragged under a bus, but the bus backed up and ran over me several times. But it's good now, so that's all that matters."

Langdon was staring at Sarah, his intense blue eyes focused on Sarah's face. Marilyn noticed the look on Langdon's face and nudged the young man. "Langdon, you look like you want to get a room with Sarah here. I know, she's beautiful. If I swung that way, I'd look at her the same way."

Sarah felt her cheeks get red. No matter how many times people told her how gorgeous she was, she never got used to it. Or welcomed it, for that matter. Especially not now. She was trying to get a responsible, serious position on the school board. The last thing she wanted was for people to look at her and think she couldn't be a substantial person because of how she looked. She had a Master's degree from Berkeley for the love of God. She was much more than a pretty face and long legs, but she had difficulty convincing people of that fact.

Langdon's spell was finally broken, for he stopped staring at her long enough to tell her that he would contribute a hundred thousand dollars to her campaign. "I'm giving you this money not just because I find you damn attractive but also because I think you'll be a very good school board member."

Max rolled his eyes at the guy. "That's nice you're going to contribute a hundred thousand dollars to Sarah's campaign. But you can't give her more than $1000, so nice try."

Sarah looked over at Max, who was glaring at Langdon. Sarah didn't know why Max was giving Langdon the stink eye, but it was unmistakable. Max looked like he wanted to kick Langdon's ass. Sarah wondered if there was some bad blood between the two of them.

It was Langdon's turn to roll his eyes. "$1000? That's the limit? That's lame."

"Be that as it may," Max said in a hostile tone. "That's the law, so them's the breaks."

"Okay, then. I'll get 100 of my friends to give her a thousand dollars, and she'll have enough money to railroad everybody else out of the race."

Sarah tried to laugh it off, but the two men looked like they were about to come to blows, and she had no idea why. "That would be great! Everybody can just go home now because it sounds like my entire campaign's about to be financed."

Max tugged on Sarah's arm. "Come out to the terrace with me, okay?"

Langdon shrugged his shoulders, and Sarah and Max made their way through the crowd to the marble terrace just off the enormous living room. There was a fountain on the stairs, and Sarah could hear the waves rolling in from the beach.

"What's going on?" Sarah asked Max. "You looked like you were about to go Bruce Lee on that guy."

"He thinks he's going to somehow buy a date from you,

and you gotta be careful. If you accept a lot of money from these rich guys, you'll be in hot water with the election commission."

"I'm well aware of the campaign finance laws. And I'm a grown-ass woman. I can take care of myself. Langdon's not the first rich guy who thought he could buy me, and he won't be the last."

Max went over to the marble balustrade and put his hands on it. He looked down as if he was struggling with composing himself. He just shook his head. "Just be careful."

"I will. But you seemed to have a problem with him. You guys know each other?"

"Nope. Never met the guy in my life. Why?"

"It's just that you looked at him like you wanted to kick his ass. For no reason, I guess. I mean, he was just trying to be generous. There's no reason to act like he just tried to kill your dog."

He swallowed hard. "Just be careful, that's all."

Sarah thought he was acting strange. Like he was jealous or something. And, all at once, Sarah wondered if Max harbored feelings for her. She already thought she was harboring feelings for him. Now she had to wonder if he felt the same way.

"Okay. Now, what do you say I go back in there, and glad hand like I'm supposed to do here?" Sarah asked. "Marilyn put this shindig together for me in record time. The least I can do is meet my possible donors."

"Of course. I'm sorry. I shouldn't have acted that way around that guy."

"No biggie." And then Sarah went back through the French doors, where the party was in full swing. It was an open bar, and everybody at the party seemed to know that Marilyn's affair wouldn't be a stuffy one. The band playing was a jazz band, but it was more modern jazz, much like the music played by John Legend's group in the movie *La La Land*, so the band didn't just feature horns and saxophones but also guitars.

Marilyn came up to Sarah. "I'm itching to get up there with that band. They're playing my song."

And then Marilyn got up on the stage, strapped on a guitar, and high-fived the current lead singer. The singer smiled and handed Marilyn the microphone. Marilyn grinned back, and the band started to play the Amy Winehouse classic *Back to Black*. As Marilyn sang the song, Sarah felt slightly blown away by the woman. Her voice was smoky, strong, silky, and deep. Her cadence and phrasing for the song lent it a fresh tone.

Sarah loved Amy Winehouse and thought it was tragic about what happened to her at such a young age. Sarah had Amy Winehouse's first CD, *Frank*, at home and *Back to Black* and played them so often that she knew every word to every song on both CDs. And, no doubt, Marilyn was doing justice to the song.

Sarah looked over at Max, who was standing next to her. "Did you know she was such a great singer?" Sarah asked him.

"I've always heard she was. That was how she met Liam. He came to a nightclub, and she was on stage singing, and he knew he would marry her from the first note. Or, so the story goes."

Sarah smiled and swayed to the music as the band started on another song by Joss Stone, the English blue-eyed soul singer who was another of Sarah's favorites.

She turned to talk to Max again, but Langdon was

beside her instead of Max. "She's amazing, isn't she?" he asked her.

"Oh my God, she is! She missed her calling because she could be a superstar on the stage with that voice and those mad guitar skills."

Langdon nudged Sarah a little. "So, what do you say to dinner with me? I'd like to learn some more about your positions." How he said the word "positions" left no imagination on exactly what positions he was talking about.

Sarah looked over at Max, who was on her other side and shooting Langdon stink-eye bullets. Yes, it definitely looked like Max was jealous.

"No. No offense, but I think I know what positions you're talking about, and I'm not interested."

Langdon raised an eyebrow. "Your loss."

The party wore on, and, by the end of the evening, it was getting just a bit out of hand. Even though it was only April, so the night air was not exactly sweltering, half the party ended up in the pool, fully clothed. At some point, Sarah was pushed into the pool and realized it was surprisingly warm. Of course, it was heated, but Sarah still thought it was a bit cool to be taking a dip.

But a dip was exactly what she ended up taking. Not that she chose that, but Langdon had playfully pushed her in.

And the second Sarah was pushed into the pool, Langdon jumped in after her, and so did Max. Langdon put his arms around her and attempted to kiss her. However, Sarah turned her cheek away.

And then she felt a pair of arms wrap around her waist

and pull her away from Langdon. The arms belonged to Max, and they were strong and muscular. She was pressed up against his chest, which was just as hard and firm as his arms. She sighed as she started to feel the tingling she hadn't felt with anybody since... she realized she might not have ever felt that kind of tingling.

"Let's get out of here," he said in her ear.

She said nothing but just nodded.

She got out of the pool, and Max followed her closely. And then, she grabbed a microphone that was about 100 feet away from the pool. "I want to thank everybody for coming this evening. It looks like this fundraiser was a smashing success, and I think I'll be well on my way to representing all of you on the school board. I wanted all of you to know how much I appreciate your support, and just know that when I get a position on the board, I'll be fighting hard for our students to learn the true history of this country and for controversial books to stay both in the library and in the curriculum. Our students will learn about all the diverse voices that shaped our country. That's my promise to you."

Everybody in and around the pool started to clap after Sarah's speech. Sarah found Marilyn to thank her for hosting the fundraiser and found her standing up on the stage, doing shots with the other band members.

"Marilyn, Max and I are leaving. But I wanted to thank you again for having this fundraiser. I can't tell you how helpful this will be for my campaign. I think I'll have enough money to properly fund it now, thanks to you."

Marilyn waved her hand dismissively at Sarah, then gave her a big hug. "I did nothing. I just threw a party, which is what I do best. You did the rest, lady. I saw you out there talking to people, and everybody was impressed with you. I know you're gonna do a great job on that school board."

"Thank you. And, by the way, you have an amazing voice, and you can play a mean guitar. Do you miss performing regularly?"

"Why do you think I have these parties? They're really just excuses for me to sing my heart out for a captive audience. But yes, I miss my band and riffing to different crowds all over the country. But this is the next best thing."

The two ladies hugged again, and Sarah reminded Marilyn about joining her and the ladies for their next wine fest. Marilyn eagerly confirmed she would be there.

And then Sarah waved goodbye to everybody and followed Max out of the pool area and onto the beach.

The two walked to the water's edge and stopped on the shore. Sarah could feel the heat still coming from Max's direction. That evening, she caught him staring at her whenever she wasn't standing next to him. And his face was unmistakable as he looked at her at that party – he desired her. And she felt the same way about him.

"That was a fun party," Sarah said lightly. "I think it was a great success, as Marilyn raised a lot of money for me."

"Yeah," Max said. His hands were in his pockets, and he looked out on the surf. "Looks like you're going to make it on the board. And I'm going to have to ironically oppose you in most of your positions. At least positions you're taking on the censorship thing."

Sarah didn't want to talk about censorship, the school board, or any of that. She just hungered for his pillowy lips to devour her own. She hungered for that like she hadn't hungered for anything in a long time. She could hear her heart beating in her own ears. And, when she put her hand to her chest, she could feel it. *Thump thump thump thump.*

"Max," Sarah began. Her voice was hoarse, and she felt embarrassed that her level of desire was coming out in the cadence and tone of her voice. "Let's not talk about the censorship thing right now. I want to talk about what's happening between you and me."

Max looked at Sarah. "Sarah, you're a drop-dead beautiful woman. But there's a cage around my heart. You don't know what damage you're dealing with here."

The two of them started to walk along the edge of the beach. Sarah didn't know what to do with the limited information Max had just given her. So, he found her attractive. That was at least nice to know. Ordinarily, Sarah could take for granted that most men would find her attractive. But Max was so inscrutable that Sarah didn't know what to think of him.

"What caused you to build the cage around your heart?" Sarah asked him.

"A man. A man who took away my faith in humanity. He also caused me to see that not every book in the library is fit for people to read. Believe it or not, I was once like you. I thought that words, ideas, great and powerful authors were our society's backbone. I never believed that any book should the censored, either. But all that changed about two years ago."

Sarah saw the look in his eye – a look of hurt and despair – and she immediately felt for him. She instinctively grabbed his hand. It was warm and just a bit calloused. "Who was it? Who could cause you to lose faith and completely change your beliefs?"

He took a deep breath, but he didn't drop her hand. In fact, he squeezed it a little bit. "It's not something I talk about easily. In fact, it's not something I talk about at all."

The two of them walked along in silence. The ocean

was wild that night – the waves were huge, crashing one after another on the shore. It seemed as if there was a storm at sea. Sarah could feel a similar storm brewing behind Max's green eyes.

Sarah didn't know how to get him to open up to her. She knew what she was going to have to do, of course. She was going to have to Google Max's name - surprisingly, she hadn't done that yet. And she was going to have to see if there was anything she could find out on the internet about what Max was talking about.

"You know, I bid on that Vegas trip during the silent auction. And I won!" Sarah was desperate to change the subject, so that was her way of doing that.

Max smiled and then put his strong arm around Sarah. "Congrats. I'm sure you and whoever you take will have a good time. Where are you going to stay? I have always loved staying at the Bellagio. I like to do it in style when I go to Vegas."

"I guess so. I love the Bellagio, but I also love the Venetian. I love the paintings in that hotel. It's like it's the next best thing to actually being in Italy."

Italy was actually a country Sarah really loved. She loved its history. She was fascinated by all the homages to ancient Roman gods and goddesses sprinkled around the gorgeous nation's metropolises. She loved the countryside – the mountains, the valleys where grapes grew wild, the fishing villages, the Amalfi coast where buildings were built right into the rocks.

And she really loved the Vatican. Sarah was never religious, mainly because she was never brought up in any one religion. Her mother was a proud atheist, who now seemed to be more agnostic as she grew older, and Sarah was never exposed that much to any one church. That said, the majesty of Vatican City took her breath away. And part of the reason why she was so attracted to the Vatican was the magnificent artwork. The Venetian in Las Vegas had similar artwork to what she saw in the Vatican, which was why she loved the hotel so much. That was why she tried to stay in the hotel whenever she went to Vegas.

Most people saw Vegas as being the height of kitsch - after all, this was a city where there was a tiny Brooklyn Bridge, a miniature Eiffel Tower, a small Statue of Liberty, a miniature pyramid - but Sarah always appreciated the city for what it was. To her, all that was considered kitschy in Vegas was more of an homage, a way to bring the world to the masses instead of representing cheap knockoffs of the real things.

Sarah considered the Venetian to be no different. In addition to having some of the most beautiful artwork this side of the Vatican, the hotel also featured indoor gondolas with stereotypical men in Italian gondola uniforms, Roman columns etched in gold leaf, and Roman-inspired balconies. Yes, all this Italian-inspired luxury was employed for only one reason, to separate the masses from their money at the gambling tables. However, Sarah still appreciated it on a different level.

"You've been to Italy?" Max asked her.

"A time or two." Sarah realized she didn't want to tell Max about her previous life. She didn't want to talk about all her traveling with Nolan. It was like that was another Sarah. That Sarah was trapped in a very bad relationship with a very controlling man. And Sarah felt if she opened that vault, she would have to relive the caged-animal feelings she felt when she was in that relationship with Nolan. So, Sarah was going to downplay her global exploits.

"Me too," Max said. "I really loved that country myself.

And, you're right. The Venetian gives me a kind of nostalgia about my trips to Italy."

As they walked along, Sarah tried hard to hold in the question she wanted to ask him. It was too soon to ask him to go on a trip, yet she wanted to share a hotel room with him. She wanted to hear him breathing next to her as she fell asleep. She wanted to imagine what it would be like if the two of them were somehow forced to share a bed.

Finally, Sarah could hold it in no more. "If you came with me, I could probably write off the Vegas trip as a business expense." She was making up an excuse on the fly, and she didn't quite know how simply inviting him along to the trip meant that she could write it off.

He smiled. "What do you mean?"

"Well, I could say I'm taking you on the Vegas trip because I'm looking for donors. Or maybe I can say I'm taking you on the trip to thank you for running my campaign."

Sarah was embarrassed about how lame the excuses sounded to her. Looking for donors in a Vegas casino? Taking him as a way of showing gratitude? Any IRS agent worth his salt would laugh at her if she tried to justify the Vegas trip as a business expense on those grounds.

And, really, she should take one of her friends, or Ava. They'd all have a good time together, doing the town. They'd probably go to magic shows, see the Chippendales and hoot and holler at them, or maybe catch a concert. There was so much to do and see in that town, and she knew she'd have fun with Ava, Quinn, and Hallie.

But, for some reason, she was determined for Max to go with her.

He smiled. "You sold me. I'm only going to go with you, of course, because I want you to be able to write the trip off.

So, we'll have to try to hit up a big donor there. I have some contacts out in Vegas I can call."

Sarah realized that she might not have been as off-base as she thought. If Max called in favors from some heavy-hitting friends in Vegas, she could write off the trip. She thought it was amusing that her ruse might work to her advantage in the fundraising game.

But, more importantly, she could get to know him better during the three-day trip.

"Okay. I guess it's a done deal. Is it going to be a problem with your farm?"

"No. I have somebody I can call to take over the farm operation for the few days we're going to be gone. And I can also get this person to take over the weekly meet and greet I do with interested people who want to learn about the farm."

"Good. That's good to hear." Sarah suddenly felt tongue-tied. She wasn't used to that feeling. She was so used to having the upper hand with any member of the opposite sex. "So, we'll be heading to Vegas in a couple of days. I hope I'm not giving you too short of notice. I can take the trip anytime, but I am really kind of itching to get out of this town for a little while. I'm used to going to the West Coast to visit wineries, but I haven't had a trip like that for a while, so I'm dying to leave Nantucket and just have some fun."

Max looked at her and smiled. "It'll be fun. And God knows I probably could use some fun of my own."

Sarah and Max walked along the shore together for the next few hours. It was easy and comfortable. It was safe. Sarah had never really had this kind of easy rapport with a man before – the comfort you feel when you can walk along with somebody and not talk the whole time but still feel comfortable in the silence.

And Sarah wondered if this was what falling in love felt like. It'd been so long since she had fallen in love with somebody like she felt when she first met Nolan. Of course, her love and affection for her former boyfriend dried up and became something much darker. But it was good for the first couple of years with Nolan.

And that was in the back of her mind as she thought about grabbing Max's hand as they walked along the sand under the new moon. It was so good with Nolan for a while, and then it was so wrong.

That was why Sarah was still afraid of falling in love.

Because love always had the potential to turn on a dime.

Chapter Nineteen

Ava

Christopher wasn't quite ready to tell Ava that night about his deep, dark secret. But he promised her he would, so Ava arranged for him to come over and visit her the next night.

She called an emergency meeting with the ladies because she felt so out of sorts about the entire thing. She had to talk it through with somebody because she was afraid she'd get sucked into Chris's web if she didn't get a different perspective. And that was the last thing she wanted.

The very last thing.

So, that Saturday evening, she hosted Quinn, Hallie and Sarah. They had the usual bottle of wine, and she made dinner for them - ginger fish with a side of whipped cauliflower. Ginger fish was actually one of the things that her mother used to make her that she craved. Her mom was not that good of a cook. Most of the time, they ate out when she was growing up. After all, her mom was a federal judge, so she wasn't around much and didn't have a lot of energy to cook and clean. But when she made something Ava loved, Ava appreciated it. And the ginger fish was something she always loved.

It was a simple dish consisting of fish marinated in ginger, soy sauce, olive oil, garlic, and sesame oil, then steamed. A ginger sauce with sesame oil, soy sauce, coconut vinegar, and ginger was poured over the fish before serving. The fish was fresh, the Asian-inspired sauce was delectable, and the ladies appreciated the meal.

"Okay, sugar, out with it. What's going on with you?" Quinn asked Ava after they finished eating.

Ava let out a large breath. And then she took a gulp of her wine. "Christopher is going to finally come clean to me about some huge secret he has. I'm freaking out about it, but I shouldn't be. I've left the man behind. Completely. He's been in the past for so long that I stopped caring about him and anything he's had to say or do. And that's been healthy for me. I mean, he betrayed me so thoroughly. Why do I care what he has to say?"

Ava shook her head. She never thought in a million years that she'd ever start to care about Christopher again. Yet, here she was, with conflicted feelings. She was starting to really care about the man again. Her feelings went beyond simply feeling sorry for him, which was the only feeling she had before. And the one thing she didn't want was to have her nascent soft feelings for the man blossom into full-blown love. She was terrified just because Chris had given her no reason to trust him.

Sarah patted Ava on the shoulder. "Don't spin out just yet. Just listen to him, and figure out what he's about. Listen to the big secret, and then decide if you can live with it. None of us know what it is just yet, so we can't give you advice on how to handle it. As your sister, I can only tell you that I'll support you no matter what. I just don't want you to make a mistake because your heart is so tender. You're like me - you root for the underdog. And I feel if Christopher comes out with a sad story, you'll get sucked in again. Just step back before you decide anything."

"I agree with Sarah," Hallie said. "You can't make a decision until you get the full story."

Ava knew the ladies were right. She was spinning out before she knew what she was spinning about. Maybe what Christopher would tell her would be something she could live with. Maybe it would be something that would be exculpatory, as they say in law. In other words, maybe he could tell her something that would exonerate him somewhat.

And, if he did, what would that mean? Would Ava ever decide to take him back? Could she go back? That was the real question. She really enjoyed her life. She was making it everything she wanted it to be and calling the shots. Every shot. She didn't have to answer to anybody, and there was something to be said for that.

What would happen if she took Christopher back? How would her life change?

Ava knew the answer to that question. If she took Christopher back, all of a sudden, she would have to clear all of her decisions with him. And she wasn't anxious to do that. Not for Christopher. Not for anybody.

That was one of the reasons why Deacon was so attractive to her. She liked him and enjoyed spending time with him, but, at the same time, she knew she could keep her relationship with Deacon in a box. Deacon would never tell her she couldn't do this or that with the bed-and-breakfast, for instance. Deacon was never going to get pouty about how much time she wanted to spend with her friends and sister. If she wanted to take off a mental health day and watch Netflix from morning until night, she wouldn't have to ask Deacon if that was okay.

But, if Christopher came back, she would be married again. She was going to have to actually share her life with somebody again. And she didn't want that. If there was one thing she'd learned in these past few years, it was that she really liked her independence. She valued it. She cherished it. Maybe she was a little bit lonely, but not really. Her life was full, and she didn't necessarily need a man to complete it.

That was why Ava was so frightened of Christopher, if she were perfectly honest with herself. Because if she allowed Christopher to come back, that would mean the divorce would be on hold. Maybe indefinitely. There would be no telling Christopher that he could just live somewhere else, and the two of them could casually date. That would be ridiculous, considering they were still married. And that was something that Ava just didn't want to get herself sucked into.

So, a big part of her wanted Christopher's secret to be some kind of a dealbreaker. Something they couldn't come back from. Something that would make Ava say, once and for all, that Christopher was her past. And it was time to get on with the divorce.

"Well, as usual, you ladies have talked me down. Now, Sarah, what is going on with your hot campaign manager?" Sarah had told Ava earlier that day about the party. It sounded like Sarah had a ball, and she raised a lot of money for her campaign. She was going to be able to get a storefront, maybe hire some people to canvas and phone bank and just help her get her name out there. But, Ava sensed there was a much bigger story. Sarah was burying the lede when she talked about the party.

Ava had a feeling her sister was falling in love.

When Sarah's face flushed bright red after Ava asked the question about Max, Ava's suspicions were confirmed. She smiled. She wanted, more than anything else in her life, for her sister to be happy. Ava knew just how unhappy Sarah had been with Nolan for the past 20 years. Sarah managed to get to the age of 54 without accomplishing a lot she hoped she would in her life – a family, true love, a career in architecture that was fulfilling. And the reason why Sarah didn't experience these things was because of Nolan.

So Ava hoped Sarah could find some true happiness. After all she went through, she deserved it.

"I don't know," Sarah said. "It's complicated. I think he's not wanting to get involved with me, for whatever reason. I think he thinks I'm some kind of a social justice leftist commie warrior." Sarah laughed lightly. "At any rate, we're going to Vegas together, so maybe I can figure out what's going on with the guy."

"Vegas?" Quinn said, laughing. "You don't know how you feel about the guy, but you're taking him on a trip?" She shook her head. "You're a braver gal than I am. I'll give you that."

Quinn was still on the fence with Asher, the attorney who was madly in love with her. She never warmed to the guy, even though he was perfect on paper. But they were casually dating, and Quinn, like Ava, preferred it that way because she was just too set in her ways to want to share her life with another person.

Still, Ava thought if Quinn ever met the guy who rocked her world, she'd probably change her tune. And, who knows? Maybe Ava would be the same way if there was somebody else like Deacon who made her heart turn upside down and inside out. But, for now, Ava was happy on her own. And Quinn was much the same way.

"I know," Sarah said. "Trust me, I wonder if I know what I'm doing. I'm leading with my heart, which I did before with Nolan, and look where that got me. That was the single biggest mistake of my entire life. If it weren't for Nolan, I'd probably still be working at that architecture firm in Los Angeles, hopefully setting the architectural world on fire. I might've become the next Zaha Hadid."

Zaha Hadid was an Iraqi architect widely considered the greatest female architect of all time. She designed everything from opera houses, museums, and sports stadiums to skyscrapers. Sarah told Ava how much she admired Hadid and felt so envious that Hadid could accomplish so much, while Sarah herself was cut down at the beginning of her architecture career just because she wanted to follow a man around the world.

"Well, sis, go ahead and lead with your heart," Ava said. "It might not work out. Then again, it might. But know this. Whether you lead with your heart or your head, you can make a big mistake either way. But you could also see it work out either way. But when you lead with your heart, I think you have a better chance of coming out on top."

The ladies clinked their wine glasses, and Ava took a big sip.

Ava and Sarah seemed to be in the same place at that point. Both of them trying to decide if it was right to let a man back into their lives. Both of them very unsure.

Ava thought she knew the right answer for herself.

And she was going to make a final decision the next night when she talked to Christopher.

She only hoped the decision she made was the right one.

Chapter Twenty

Ava

The next night, Ava had Christopher over to her home. She invited him for drinks on her veranda, not for dinner. She didn't want to bother with the whole formality of cooking something for him and didn't want to order something in, either. So, she just had an early sandwich and salad, and Christopher joined her for the usual bottle of wine.

Christopher looked extremely nervous. "What if I don't tell you what I need to tell you?" he asked her. He looked like he wanted to be anywhere but there. Like he wanted the floor to swallow him whole, and that would be a better fate than what he was about to face. That was the look he had.

"It's pretty simple. You can tell me or not. But if you don't tell me, we have no chance. I'll file for divorce tomorrow. If you tell me, who knows? Maybe we can get past it, maybe we can't."

Ava didn't tell him she was 90% sure she would file for

divorce, no matter what he told her. Still, there was that 10% of her that wanted to see where it all went.

But, if he chose not to say anything, she was 100% sure she would file for divorce the next day. So, if he wanted to have any shot with her, he needed to tell her. Let the chips fall where they may.

"Okay. Here goes." Chris took a gulp of his wine and looked green. Like he was going to go over to the railing and puke onto the beach below. "I had a child."

Oh. That was something Ava was not really prepared to hear from him. "When?"

Christopher closed his eyes. "About 10 years ago. I had another life, another family. They lived on the Upper East side, across the park from us."

Ava narrowed her eyes. "What do you mean you had another life?"

"I mean, I married this other woman." He took a deep breath. "I was a bigamist."

Ava just stared at him. This was not on her bingo card, to say the very least.

And then, she burst out laughing.

Christopher looked at Ava like she had grown another head. "What's so funny?"

Ava was still laughing so hard that she couldn't get the words out. "You," she finally sputtered. "Of all the things you could've told me, this was the one thing I never would've thought would come out of your mouth. You were married to somebody else while you were married to me? I mean, I saw a farce like this on stage where a man was married to two different women, and it was the funniest comedy I've ever seen. Apparently, I was living one of the lead parts, and I didn't even know it."

Ava was referring to a sex farce called *Run for Your Wife*, a play she once saw in a dinner theater. In that play, a cab driver had two different wives. The fun began when the two wives were almost going to find out about each other, and the husband's shenanigans in making sure they didn't were the crux of the play.

Years ago, she'd also read a novel called *The Pilot's Wife* by Anita Shreve. In that book, a pilot's wife discovers after her husband crashes and dies that he had a secret wife and family overseas.

In other words, Ava was familiar with the concept of having two different families and two different marriages. She just didn't think it would ever happen to her.

And then she thought about Hallie's earlier speculation, which was a throwaway, almost a joke. Hallie had said maybe Chris married an old lady in France, and the lady died, which was how Christopher got the money to pay her back. Ava's reply that she didn't know exactly how bigamists got caught suddenly seemed prescient.

And the thought that she and Hallie were making a joke about this very issue made Ava start to laugh again.

Oh, this was just too good.

"I don't know why you think this is so funny."

"I'll tell you why it's funny. It's hilarious because there was a tiny, minuscule part of me that thought maybe the two of us could make a go of it again. Now I know it's not going to happen, and I'm so relieved."

Chris seemed indignant. "Relieved? Relieved? Why are you relieved?"

"Because. I didn't want to have to agonize about a decision about whether or not to take you back. And if you would've told me something that made me see you in a different light, I probably would've just ended up confused about what I wanted to do about you. I would've gone back and forth, back and forth, weighing the pros and cons, as I do. And maybe I would've made the wrong decision, which would've been taking you back for any reason. As it is, though, that door is slammed shut. Full stop. End of story. And I can't tell you how relieved you've made me feel."

Christopher looked at his glass of wine, and then he, too, started to laugh. "I didn't think I'd ever find humor in the situation, but you're making me see it. It is ridiculous if you think about it."

"It is. How did you manage to have another family, by the way? Did she know about me?"

Christopher just kind of smiled. "Well, if you recall, I started taking a lot of business trips about 10 years ago. Do you remember that?"

"Now that you mention it, I do remember that." Of course, Ava didn't think anything of Christopher suddenly traveling for work much more than he was before. He had a job that involved him going to different countries all the time. He traveled for work a lot the entire time they were married, and, now that Ava thought about it, his travel schedule did amp up quite a bit about 10 years ago.

"Well, when I was traveling for work, I usually was actually traveling. But sometimes, when I said I was traveling, I was spending time with my other family."

Ava tried to resist the urge to start laughing again. Oh, she was so naïve. And if she had known at the time what Christopher was up to, she would've been devastated.

As it was, she was merely amused by it all.

"Go on," Ava said, trying hard to stifle another round of giggles. "I think all this has to do with your breakdown, and I just need to know the entire story."

Christopher took a deep breath. "My child, Heather, she died. About seven years ago. Leukemia."

And, just like that, Ava no longer felt the desire to laugh. Now, she just saw a man in pain. And, even though Ava was now 100% sure she would never take him back, it didn't mean he wasn't a human to her. He was. And she really didn't hate him. No matter what, she wouldn't hate him. After all, hate is just another side of the coin from love. You have to feel passionately about somebody to hate him or her. Ava had no passionate feelings for Chris, so she would never hate him.

That was when she knew for sure she'd moved past him. He'd just told her he'd betrayed her in an ultimate way, and she didn't care. But she could still muster up sympathy for the man.

In other words, she was in a good place with Christopher. She could divorce him, probably keep him in her life as a friend. But she didn't have to worry about upending her life to make way for his.

And that was incredibly freeing for her.

"Chris, I'm so sorry. So sorry to hear that. You must've loved your little girl very much. And I guess she was your only biological child, making it all the harder."

Chris just nodded. "She was the light of my life. A beautiful little girl, and so intelligent and sweet."

Ava found herself putting her hand on his shoulder and squeezing it. He was now a friend, nothing more, and she was going to comfort him.

"Go on," Ava said in a soft voice.

Chris took a deep breath. "She died the same year my dad killed himself, and I just went off the deep end. I think my bipolar was in remission for many years. Well, maybe not in remission exactly, but it was manageable. But when I had those two stressors happen to me in such a short period, I lost it. I turned to gambling because I might've put a gun in my mouth and pulled the trigger if I didn't. Gambling took my mind off Heather and my dad. And even when I started to lose all that money, I focused on that, not on the double whammies."

"So, the thrill of the gambling was what kept you alive during the darkest days of your life," Ava said. "And then when you really started to lose-"

Chris nodded. "Yes. It was devastating when I started to lose, but it was somehow easier for me to focus on my gambling losses than on the loss of my child and my father. And I had such complicated feelings about my dad. Feelings that were never resolved because I could never confront him while he was alive about what he did to my sister. And I just had so many guilt feelings, wrapped up with overwhelming grief, wrapped up with the lowest self-esteem you could possibly imagine. I was in such a dark hole."

"And where are you now? Where is your headspace right now?"

Chris smiled. "Believe it or not, it's better. Especially now. You know my deep, dark secrets. I paid you back. I'm in recovery. And the overwhelming grief I felt about Heather and my dad has gotten better with the passage of time. I'm finally ready to get back to the living."

"You should. Of course, we're going to have to divorce. It'll be a pain in the ass because we have so many assets together. But the lawyers will take care of it."

Chris looked resigned, but he didn't look like he was too sad about Ava telling him the divorce would have to go forward. He might've thought he wanted to get back together with Ava, but he didn't. Ava knew that by looking into his eyes. He was ready to move on without her.

They both finally had closure.

"Ava, don't let any of these revelations make you feel I didn't love you. Because I did. I loved you very much."

Ava raised an eyebrow. "Maybe you loved me. But, if you did, you didn't love me enough not to cheat on me."

"That's fair. I don't suppose it would help if I told you that my relationship with Maya, my other wife, started as a drunken one-night stand?"

"How would that help?"

"Well, it wasn't something I meant to happen. And, if she didn't get pregnant from that one-night stand, I doubt I would've ever seen her again."

"Okay," Ava said. "When you were married to her, did you sleep with her?"

"Of course," Chris said.

"Then, there's your answer. It doesn't make it better that it started out as a one-night stand. You were cheating on me all along with this woman. But you knew this, so don't even bother trying to minimize it."

Chris shrugged his shoulders. "I know."

Ava was confused about one thing, though. "I don't understand. If it was so casual, why did you marry her?"

"Because I wanted to be a true father to Heather," Chris said. "Maya made it plain to me that unless we got married, she'd do what she could to deny me custody. That was her condition, and I caved. I know. I could've taken the whole matter to court and gotten visitation. And come clean with you while I was at it. But I didn't take the right steps. I married her so I could be close to my daughter. She was my only biological child, and I would've done anything to maintain a relationship with her."

Ava could see the situation without emotion, and she understood and saw a certain logic to it all. "Why didn't you just leave me to marry her?" she asked.

Chris sighed. "Because I loved you and couldn't imagine life without you. I know it sounds twisted, but that's the truth."

Ava thought that was lame, but whatever.

"Okay. So, what happened? How did it end? Did it end at all?"

"Actually, I divorced her after Heather passed away. Or she divorced me. She told me she only married me because she wanted a father for Heather. She didn't love me. I didn't love her. So, the only thing to do was to divorce."

Ava might not have had much knowledge about the bigamist thing, but she knew the second marriage was invalid from the start. Therefore, it would've been null and void, so Christopher didn't need to formally divorce the woman. But, since Christopher didn't tell Maya he was already married, he probably did the divorce thing for show.

"So, what are you going to do now?" Ava asked.

Chris shrugged his shoulders. "Go back to New York City, and go back to my old profession. I'm in a pretty good head space right now, so I think I can pick up the pieces of my life and move on."

"I think that's a good idea," Ava said. "And you can go forward knowing we're friends. I want what's best for you. That's not me, but that's okay. It really is."

Chris had a smile on his face. "Ava, you really are the best. I don't think I could ask for a kinder wife. I know I screwed everything up."

"Don't feel bad about that," Ava said. "Listen, I doubt I'd be here if you didn't screw everything up. When this house was willed to me, I wouldn't have come here and opened up this B&B if I was still married to you. I'm not sure what I would've done with it, but it wouldn't have been that. I probably still would be living in New York City, working as an attorney, even if I probably wouldn't have been working for Collins and Lahy anymore."

Chris had a twinkle in his eye. "In other words, you owe everything to me."

"In a sense, yes," Ava said. "At any rate, everything settled out just how it was supposed to. And I'm much happier now than I ever was in New York City. So, in a way, I have to thank you for screwing me over. Because if you didn't, I would've been going along with the inertia, not wanting to rock the boat. And I don't think I'd be happy. Which I am. Insanely happy. So, go forth, and know I don't hate or resent you. I want what's best for you. I want you to be happy."

And as Ava looked into Chris's eyes, she knew she was telling him the absolute truth. There was no bad blood between them. No ill will. And it was obvious he felt the same way about her.

They couldn't be married again, but that was okay.

Ava was finally free of Christopher.

And she had never felt happier in her life.

Chapter Twenty-One

Sarah

Sarah and Max went to Vegas that Wednesday. She booked two first-class tickets and booked a stay at the Venetian. As she sat next to him on the plane, she felt giddy with excitement. It wasn't just that she loved Vegas, which she did. She always did, but she had especially fond memories of Vegas because it was in Vegas that she learned she possessed a very valuable coin.

Nolan's wife, Olivia, who he never divorced even though they had lived apart for a good 10 years before Sarah even met the man, took sympathy on Sarah because Sarah was left with nothing after Nolan's death. So, Olivia decided to make Sarah wealthy by sending her a penny.

This penny turned out to be worth almost $3 million.

Sarah, of course, was very suspicious of the penny coming through the mail. It was sent anonymously, and that particular penny, the 1943 copper penny, was often counterfeited. The issue was that, in 1943, America started using steel to make their pennies instead of copper. However, about 50 or so pennies that year were made of copper, and those pennies were worth a lot of money. So, people who thought they were being clever sometimes took 1948 copper pennies and carefully shaved off just enough of the eight to make it look like a three. Others took a steel 1943 penny and dipped it into copper.

Sarah just assumed the penny wasn't real. At least, until she went to a numismatic show at the Bellagio. There, she found out that the penny was real. And she was able to get over $2.5 million for the penny at auction. That enabled Sarah to buy her house, which went a long way toward easing Sarah's financial burdens.

So, Vegas now had a very special place in her heart. It was there that she found out she was probably going to be a millionaire.

And now, she was going to make new memories. New memories with this very handsome man who made Sara feel a little giddy.

She was so excited about the trip with Max that she had forgotten about trying to Google him to find out his big secret. She knew it was something. There were just too many clues, just too many questions. Yet, she had no idea exactly what the mystery was.

But as she sat on the plane, drinking champagne next to Max, she didn't think about it. Perhaps it was going to come out at some point, perhaps not. This trip wasn't necessarily about that. This trip was about the two of them getting to know each other better while having a lot of fun doing it.

The plane landed, and Max and Sarah got an Uber to take them to the hotel. The Uber dropped them off, they checked into their beautiful suite with a view of the city, and Sarah excitedly lay down on the bed.

Max lay down next to her, and the two of them stared at the ceiling. "What do you want to do first?" Max asked.

"Let's get dinner at some celebrity chef restaurant, and then we'll talk. While we're here, I want to see David Copperfield or maybe Criss Angel. I love illusionists and magicians. I just don't know how they can do it. It's like they really are magic, you know?"

Max grinned. "You know, you have a childlike quality I didn't know about. It's really very attractive."

"You don't know the half of it." She wanted to tell Max that her basic nature had been denied for over 20 years as she assumed the identity Nolan had wanted for her. Nolan wanted Sarah to be just so. It wasn't exactly a *Sleeping with the Enemy* situation, where he ordered her to dress, act, and look a certain way, but he definitely controlled their life. Sarah had forgotten some basic parts of herself when she was with him. Like the fact that she absolutely loved magicians.

"Well, let's get tickets for Criss Angel," Max said as he brought out his laptop. 10 minutes later, he had their seats arranged. "Just got some good seats. Now, let's go to Giada De Laurentiis' place. I'm in the mood for some good Italian, and you said you wanted to go to a celebrity chef's restaurant. So, what do you think?"

"I think that sounds amazing."

So, the two went to Giada's restaurant. The beautiful restaurant was located inside a fancy hotel called The Cromwell. It featured a gorgeous view of the Bellagio fountains, which were doing their show right when they were seated.

Sarah's mouth watered as she looked at the menu. The ravioli with lobster and lemon butter sounded good to her, as did the arugula salad with candied lemon, prosciutto ham, and Parmesan cheese.

She ordered those two things, and Max ordered the Branzino fish with ratatouille and Pomodoro. He, too, ordered the arugula salad and a bottle of wine.

"This is going to be my treat," Max said to Sarah. "You brought me on this trip, so I'm going to buy dinner and the magician and whatever else you need while you're here."

Sarah smiled. "Seriously, it's my treat to bring you here. I really wanted to get to know you better."

"No arguments," he said playfully.

The waiter came around, took their order, and brought out the wine.

Sarah looked out the window, and the Bellagio fountains were again in motion. They played every 15 minutes in the evenings, and Sarah was always fascinated by them. That was another thing about her – she appreciated the small things in life. Like how much fun it was to see those fountains dance.

Max was watching Sarah, and when she looked back at him, his look told her he felt for her the same way she felt for him.

"You love those fountains, don't you?" he asked.

"Oh, yes. It's weird how compelling they are. It's like one of the most brilliant things the hotel could've done – install some iconic fountains that everybody talks about and visits. It puts the name Bellagio on everybody's lips."

"It does." He poured some wine for himself and Sarah. "So, cheers!"

Sarah nodded her head. "What are we cheering? I mean, what are we celebrating?"

"There's no reason for us to put a label on this dinner," Max said. "It's just two people out on the town."

Sarah furrowed her brows. "Oh. I thought maybe we were celebrating my successful fundraiser. And maybe looking forward to a very successful campaign."

Max took a deep breath. "Sarah, don't get me wrong, but I really hope you don't get a position on the school board."

Sarah was confused, to say the very least. She took a big sip of her wine. "You're my campaign advisor. I don't understand."

"I've come to realize you're a force to be reckoned with," Max said. "You have this charisma. People are drawn to you. People listen to you. You have this way about you that makes people want to bend over backward to do what you say. I saw that at the fundraiser. Everybody was charmed by you."

Sarah sensed a backhanded compliment in his words. There was definitely a "but" coming.

Sarah didn't have to wait long for that "but" to make itself known.

"Okay. So I'm a force to be reckoned with, and people are drawn to me and want to do what I say. You're telling me I'm a leader, which would seem to be a good thing. What am I missing?"

Max finished off his wine and then stared at Sarah. "You're going to get your agenda passed. And I think that's harmful to our kids. I'm sorry. I probably should've never taken you on. I guess I underestimated you. But I saw how people were drawn to you at that fundraiser. I know you'll get whatever you want on the school board."

Sarah clasped her hands in front of her. "Again, where is the problem?"

"A book killed my daughter," Max blurted out. "The words, the vile, hateful words in this book fed this crazy bastard. His name was Lucas McMorrow. He was influenced by this book called *The Turner Diaries*."

Sarah sat back. She was getting to the nub of why Max believed the way he did. "I know about that book. It deals with a race war and the genocide of all nonwhite people worldwide. It's the book that inspired Timothy McVeigh. It's the book that led to the dragging death of James Byrd in Texas. It's the book that far-right extremists use as their Bible."

Max nodded. "Yes. That's right. So you know what kind of effect it has on people."

Sarah sighed. "What exactly happened? How did that book lead to the death of your daughter?"

Max looked out the window, seeing the fountains go off once again. "My wife, Elaine, died about 15 years ago. Breast cancer. We had adopted a little girl from Africa. We named her Tumaini, which is the Swahili word for hope. My wife was diagnosed with breast cancer soon after the adoption went through. She had that HER-2 type, so it was very aggressive. She died within a year."

Sarah took his hand. She knew how he felt, in a way, because Nolan had died. She knew what it meant to be with a dying person. It was brutal, something she wouldn't wish on anyone.

"I'm so sorry to hear that," Sarah said. "So, Julia is 13..."

"Right. Julia was born through a surrogate. After she was diagnosed, Elaine and I agreed to fertilize some embryos, so she could have a legacy. But, at the time she died, Tumaini was my only light. She was such a beautiful little girl. So smart. She was my reason for living after Elaine died. And this man took her away from me."

Sarah continued to put her hand on Max's and looked into his eyes. "What happened?"

Max swallowed hard. "I had a bit of a name in D.C. You know, I managed quite a few campaigns for many Democrats. Both for the House and Senate. That was my entire job. And apparently this man, this Lucas McMorrow evil man, I hate even saying his name because it makes me want to vomit every time I do, found out I had an adopted daughter from Africa."

Sarah narrowed her eyes. "Lucas McMorrow. He ran for Senate. I remember that now."

Max nodded his head. "Right. He wasn't running as a Republican. He was running as an independent. And he was able to raise all this money from these white supremacists, which was why he was able to mount a real campaign."

"So, he found you had a daughter from Africa, and..."

Max took a deep breath. "He had a lot of followers. Followers who hated me for two reasons. First, I was putting out a lot of ads for my client against him and his beliefs. They were hard-hitting ads, and it was unmistakable what kind of person Lucas was. So that was one reason why his followers despised me. I told the public the truth about the man. The other reason why his followers hated me was because I had an African daughter."

Sarah was starting to remember the story. The kidnapping. The ransom. The desperate father who would do anything to get his daughter back. The child found at the bottom of a ravine after the desperate father paid the ransom.

Sarah felt her heart stop. Max was the father at the center of all this tragedy. "Oh, Max, I'm so sorry. I'm so, so, so sorry." Sarah put her hand on his. "I remember the story now. Your daughter was kidnapped. And murdered."

Max nodded his head. "Yes. She was, and it was because she was African, and that bastard felt she didn't deserve to live. The reason why that sick bastard felt that way about her was because of that book he read. The reason why all those people died in the Oklahoma City bombing was because of that same book. I realized that words can do an incredible amount of damage. Words can be dangerous. Words can lead people to hate, kill, bomb federal buildings."

Max now had tears in his eyes.

The waitress brought their food and asked if they wanted anything else. They both waved their hand at her. Neither one of them wanted to deal with the waitress at that point.

"Max," Sarah said in as gentle a voice as possible. "I understand. But you know that that book isn't available in any school library. And, in fact, I don't think the book is available in most public libraries. And, at any rate, the books the school wants to ban are nothing like that book. They're classics. Pulitzer Prize winners. Powerful books. *The Turner Diaries* is nothing but a trash book. A vile screed that does nothing but take Hitler's ideas and put them into a novel. What Hitler wanted was exactly what that book was about – a worldwide genocide of all Jews and nonwhites. That's nothing like the books on the list to be banned."

Max angrily slammed his fist on the table. "I know that! Don't you think I know that? I can't help how I feel. I'm sorry. I've had a lot of therapy on this, and I know you're right. My head knows you're right. But my heart and soul feel that certain books are just dangerous. Certain ideas are just dangerous."

Sarah was going to still try to talk some sense into him.

"Max, here's the other thing. Those people inspired by that book were probably drawn to it because they were already hateful. It's not like people with love in their heart are going to read that book and suddenly decide they were going to become a hateful genocidal white supremacist."

Max rolled his eyes. "Again, you're talking to me like I'm five years old. I know what you're saying. What I'm saying is that you take a troubled loser and expose him or her to hateful ideology, and you're just lighting a match. You're pouring gasoline."

Sarah drank the rest of her wine and shook her head. "Max, I understand. I understand why you left D.C. Why you left the political game. I would too if that happened to me. And I can even understand why you're so adamant about keeping students away from certain books. But I hope you know that I have the best interests of our students in mind. And, of course, I'd never be in favor of *The Turner Diaries* or *Mein Kampf* or any hate-filled book to be in the school library. I just want to make sure students can read the powerful classics. That's all."

Max squared his jaw. "Let's not talk about this anymore. Let's just have a good time at the magic show. Vegas is a place that's a playground. You come here to leave your troubles behind. So let's just do that."

Sarah nodded her head and dug into her food. She was happy she got to the bottom of Max's hesitations regarding censorship. And now she knew the soft underbelly of his objections. She understood him. And she knew she would be able to turn him onto the way she was thinking.

But, for now, the subject was dropped.

The two of them ate the rest of their meal in silence.

Chapter Twenty-Two

Sarah

After the meal, Sarah and Max caught the Criss Angel show, which was as magnificent as she had imagined. She was amazed at the things he could do in his show. She felt like a little kid because, after the show, she was hyperactive. Bouncing off the walls. Just like when she was young.

After the show, they went to the casino in the Venetian. And, for some reason, both of them drank. A lot. Sarah wasn't used to that much alcohol at once, and she felt herself losing control. But they were having a great time. Sarah won some money at the craps table, and Max won some money on video poker.

So, they celebrated winning at the casino by going to a nightclub. They drank some more there. It was mainly a blur, but Sarah knew they were dancing wildly. She'd drank so much that she was becoming unaware of her surroundings. And she was starting to feel more than a little sick.

Sarah woke up in her bed in the Venetian Hotel. She had no idea how she got there. The night was a blur after the magic show. It seemed as if she went to a bar with Max, although she couldn't be sure. And maybe she won some money? Again, she couldn't be sure of that, either.

What she was sure of it was that her head was splitting open. And she felt nauseated. She ran to the bathroom and puked.

She wasn't used to drinking a lot. Why was she doing it last night? She didn't really know, except she thought that maybe she drank so much because she was in Vegas, and that's what you're supposed to do when you're in Vegas.

And then she looked around the room. Max was nowhere to be found.

Well, maybe he went to the casino again to win some more. Or maybe he went to the breakfast buffet. Sarah would've appreciated a note telling her exactly where he was. But, there was no note to be seen.

But then she looked at her finger and she saw it.

A cracker jack ring.

What did she do?

Then she saw something else that made her heart race.

A marriage license.

What the hell? She was schnockered but not that blotto. Was she?

How did this happen? Why did this happen?

Bits and pieces of the previous night started to flood her brain. The license bureau, which closed at midnight. Max urging her to hurry to get to the bureau before they closed. The 24-hour wedding chapel. The minister pronouncing them husband and wife in front of two randos they managed to drag in as witnesses.

She lay back down on the pillow and squeezed her eyes shut tight. Oh, this was embarrassing. Here she was, 53 years old, and her first marriage was a drunken quickie in Vegas. That was the kind of thing you were supposed to do when you were 23, not 53, yet that's what happened to her.

She suddenly regretted the trip to Vegas more than she ever thought she would. And, to make matters worse, she physically felt awful. She and Max had been up all night, and she had drunk more than she had in a long time.

She heard Max coming in the door. He was armed with a dozen roses. "Hey, sleepy head," he said dreamily as he sat down on the bed next to her. "How you doing?"

"Not good," she said, shaking her head. "I feel really, really sick. And we're married. How did this happen?"

He started to laugh. "It was a dare somebody made to us. And I'm never one to back down from a good double-dog dare. At least, when I'm drinking, I'm not going to back down. As for you, you seemed game. So, we did it."

"Wait. You seem like you were at least a little bit sober," Sarah said. "Unlike me."

Max just smiled and kissed her. She didn't remember kissing him last night, but she must have. At any rate, his kiss was amazing. Soft, light, pillowy like a cloud. Her body felt like it was on fire with that kiss.

"You're going to have to fill in the blanks," Sarah said. "And-"

"I know. I know. We're going to have to get it annulled as soon as possible. That won't be hard to do, considering you were inebriated at the ceremony and couldn't really consent." He looked shy. "I was teasing about the dare thing. I married you last night because I'm in love with you. And

I've been in love with you since the moment you stood up in that school board meeting and pissed me off so much."

As she looked into his eyes, Sarah realized she felt the same way about him. "In vino veritas," she said. "In wine, there's truth. I guess I probably wanted to marry you, too."

Then she remembered another reason why she agreed to marry him. Yes, she was drunk, very drunk. But she really did love him. And she wanted to become a stepmother to Julia. She so longed to be a mother, which was physically impossible for her - she'd gone into menopause 5 years prior.

Even if she wasn't post-menopausal, she still wouldn't be able to have kids at her age because it would just be too dangerous. She'd heard of women getting pregnant and delivering a baby at her age - Brigitte Nielsen, the former wife of Sylvester Stallone, was one such woman. But Sarah wouldn't want that even if it was possible.

So, being a stepmother to a great kid like Julia appealed to Sarah very much.

But she barely knew this guy. And she just moved into her home, which she loved very much.

Max kissed her on her forehead, and Sarah closed her eyes. "We don't have to live together," he said. "We can get to know each other, like a regular couple. But I'd like some security for Julia in case anything ever happens to me, and I know you'd be a great mother to her. So, I know you probably want our marriage annulled, and if that's what you want, we'll do that. But I'd like you to think about it."

Sarah opened her eyes. "Why would something happen to you?" she asked, suddenly anxious. Maybe Max married her because he was sick and wanted a mother for Julia.

Max bit his bottom lip. "I should've told you before you agreed to marry me. And, in the light of day, I feel like I manipulated you into this. But I'm sick. End stage melanoma." He chuckled. "Guess I got out in the sun too much when I was young, and I paid the price." He closed his eyes. "So, if you want our marriage annulled because you were tricked into it, I won't stand in your way."

Sarah felt her heart crash to her shoes. She finally found a man who gave her butterflies, and he was dying. She was going to have to go through it all again. She did it for Nolan. Now, she would have to do it for Max.

"Max, I-"

"Sarah, before you say anything, I need you to know something. My sister lives in Los Angeles and will let me move in with her so I can be a California resident." He paused and swallowed hard. "I'm going to get a doctor to sign off so I can die with dignity. Physician-assisted suicide. I'm not going to become your burden. But I'd like you to have custody of Julia after I go."

Sarah felt tears coming to her eyes. She was in love with this guy. But he was asking her to become a mother to a girl she barely knew, and she would have to raise her without him.

She loved the idea of being married to him and being Julia's stepmother. But raising Julia without him around would be difficult, to say the least. "If we get the marriage annulled…"

Max shook his head. "She'll go to my other sister Hannah. My sister Mary, the one who lives in California, has already told me she can't take Julia. She can't afford it. But Hannah can. She's a high-powered attorney in New York City."

Sarah saw the pain on Max's face. "Would it be okay for her to go with Hannah?" Sarah asked.

"I'd rather she not," Max said. "Hannah's a difficult

woman. Very short-tempered. Demanding. No patience. I don't want Julia to end up with her."

Sarah just shook her head and felt tears coming to her eyes. Oh, this was an impossible situation. She didn't know Julia well, but she liked what she knew about the young girl. Julia was now Emerson's best friend. Like Emerson, she was intelligent, talented, acerbic and funny.

But she was going to be raising her after her father died. Somehow, she thought that Julia was going to resent her and was going to give her headaches.

"What about your farm?" Sarah asked. Did he expect her to take the reins?

"You'll be my wife. My heir. You can do what you want with the farm after I die. I doubt you'll want to stay on the farm, although you seemed to enjoy yourself when you visited it."

Suddenly, Sarah's brain was swimming with a hundred million questions. She wasn't prepared for this. Any of this.

She was only prepared to come to Vegas to have some fun. See a magic show, have some laughs, get away. Get to know the handsome farmer/campaign advisor who was haunting her dreams. She never, ever thought she would be faced with such a decision.

Yet, she was.

"Max, I just don't know," Sarah said. "I've always wanted a child. Always. To tell you the truth, that's what's been missing in my life. Not having a kid is probably my biggest regret."

"I know," Max said. "Julia told me. Julia wants this, by the way. She really likes you."

"How did Julia know I wanted a child so much?" Sarah asked.

"Emerson told her. I guess you and Emerson have had some heart to hearts."

That was true. She and Emerson had stayed up late talking more than once. And she did admit to Emerson how much she had always longed for a child.

"So, you knew this was going to happen?"

Max took a deep breath. "I wanted it to happen, yes. I wanted to find a mother for Julia, and I've known you'd be a great choice for awhile. I want a mother who's smart, responsible, caring and independent. A good role model for her. You'd be an amazing role model. I'd die in peace if I knew you were there for her."

Sarah was a bit confused. "By the way, you were talking last night about how you were worried about my being on the school board, I never thought you wouldn't be around for much longer. I just don't understand."

"Sarah, I *am* worried about your beliefs. Just because I'm dying doesn't mean I don't think about what will happen to the kids in that school. I'm more worried than ever because I won't be around to influence kids who might turn to the dark side."

Sarah closed her eyes. She was going to have to make the decision of her life.

She really needed to talk to the ladies.

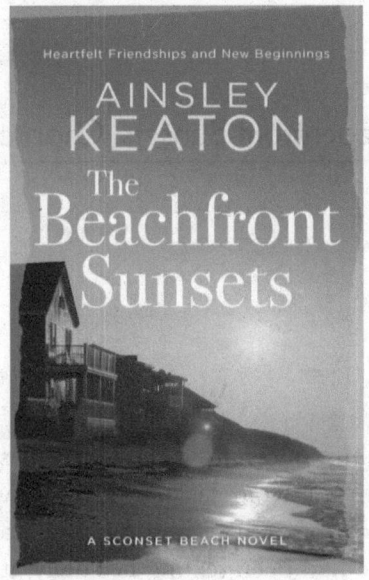

vinci-books.com/beachfront-sunsets

In the face of love, loss, and life's complexities, Sarah and Willow find solace in each other and a little magic.

Sarah embarks on a poignant final road trip with her dying love, Max, and his young daughter, Julia, creating cherished memories and finding solace in each other's company. Meanwhile, Willow reluctantly travels to Los Angeles, guided by two bickering ghosts from the 1920s, to aid her soul mate, Jackson Flynn, with her magical abilities.

Turn the page for a free preview…

The Beachfront Sunsets: Chapter One

Willow

Ever since she ran into him at the Christmas party, Willow had been trying to avoid Jackson Flynn, Ava's son. So, it had been almost 5 months, and Jackson was back in Los Angeles, but he had been texting her daily at first and then weekly. Willow didn't respond to any of its texts.

She had no desire to. Jackson was dangerous for her because he was her soulmate.

He was the one who she'd been dreaming about. Literally. He'd come into her dreams, night after night, telling her he was close. Of course, how he appeared in her dreams was different from how he actually looked.

In her dreams, he was dark-headed with long hair. And he was dressed in the style of 16th Century England, with an embroidered chemise and ruffled sleeves, a snug-fitting jacket known as a doublet, hose and a codpiece.

Sometimes. Other times, he was dressed in Victorian garb, with a top hat, long coat, vest, notched collar and breeches. His face sported the signature facial hair of the day - mutton chops.

Willow's favorites were the dreams where he appeared to her in 1920s garb. Newsboy cap, three-piece suit in brown tweed, a pocket watch, cap-toe Oxfords and a bow tie.

Still other times, he was clad in fur. In those iterations, he was hairy, stooped and spoke only in guttural grunts.

Those were just some of the ways Jackson had appeared to her. There were many, many more.

In other words, she'd gone through many lives for eons. And, apparently, there was a man in every one of those lives. The same man.

Jackson.

Of course, now that he finally made his presence known in her life, she had no interest in pursuing it further. No. If there was one thing that Willow had zero interest in, it was getting involved with a man. Any man, even her soul mate, as Jackson apparently was.

She realized that, in her previous lives, she'd given away her power. Of course. She had to. When she lived in Victorian times, she was considered her husband's property and nothing more. She was born into money in that lifetime, but that money immediately became the property of her husband from the moment she said "I do." She was a witch, then, but kept that a secret lest she be persecuted. Not that it was her husband's decision for her to live such a miserable cosseted life. It wasn't. But it was society's decision, and she had to abide.

When she lived in the 1920s, she was a feminist and a writer. She was also a powerful witch who agitated for change and spoke out about injustice perpetrated against women, blacks and other minorities. However, she was also cut down by a man in that lifetime. Not by her husband - her husband, in all her lifetimes, was good, kind and just - but by a man who dragged her into an alley and stabbed her after word got around about her abilities.

As for her life in 16th Century England...she shuddered. She remembered the rope around her neck and thinking it could've been worse. She could've been burned at the stake. But it was bad enough, and she knew she was there because of men. Specifically, the men in that country during that time and their desire to control women. Especially powerful women.

She'd lived other lives, too, many of them. And, in every one of those lives, right back to her life in the cave some hundreds of thousands of years ago, she couldn't live freely, on her own terms, because of men. She was always controlled and always had to play the dutiful woman who didn't rock the boat. The one time that she didn't play that part, her life in the 1920s, she died at 22. She was getting loud and out of her societal-imposed stricture, which proved fatal.

That was why Willow had always chosen to live life in a solitary manner. On her terms. Without having to apologize for or explain anything she did. If she wanted to spend the day shopping in the historic district, she did. If she wanted to work a spell at midnight under a full moon, she did. If she wanted to spend three whole days not sleeping and feverishly working on a sculpture that demanded to be created, she did. If she wanted to spend an entire afternoon trash-binging *Real Housewives* or the Kardashians, she did.

Mainly, though, she never had to deal with negative energies that inevitably come from any kind of relationship. She never had to absorb another person's pissy mood. She never had to walk on tiptoes, desperately trying to not disturb a drunken, snoring man like her father. That happened too many times to count.

And, of course, she never had to explain what she did. Men never got it. Women usually did. She felt a sisterhood with most women and was comfortable using her gifts around most females. But men, for some reason, mainly just thought she was strange. Not that she cared what other people thought, but it was just negativity that she didn't care to deal with.

Of course, Jackson would get it if she told him what she was. Of that, she was sure. After all, she was always a witch, wise woman, or healer in all their other lifetimes together. And in all their lifetimes together, he never seemed to mind. So she knew that this iteration wouldn't mind, either.

No matter. She still wasn't going to get involved.

Her power was her power, and she wasn't going to give away even an ounce of it. She knew that Jackson would, unwittingly or not, demand some of that power. Men always did. And in this lifetime, she was never going to give it up.

Even to her soul mate.

The Beachfront Sunsets: Chapter Two

Willow

Clara Bow was the first one to haunt Willow. "Hiya, Toots," she said in her strong Brooklyn accent. "I can't tell you how glad I am to get out of that broad's space."

She was chewing gum, her fire-engine red hair sticking up in all directions, her pencil-thin brows raised playfully, and her huge brown eyes were shining, lighting up her soft round face. Her bow-shaped lips were turned up in a huge smile. She appeared to Willow in one of her slimmer phases, as her weight tended to yo-yo during her life. She was wearing a man's shirt and tie under a skirt held up with shoulder straps.

Willow simply raised an eyebrow. "Clara Bow. What are you doing here?"

Clara Bow just rolled her eyes. "Don't I wish I knew. I got stuck with that bird because she wanted me to be there."

"Who are you talking about?"

"Zelda. She always thinks she's calling the shots. I keep

telling her to buzz off, but she don't listen to me. That dame, she thinks she's just the cat's pajamas, but I just think she's a wet blanket."

"Zelda?" Willow asked.

"Fitzgerald. You know, the broad married to that F. Scott Fitzgerald guy. I got stuck with her. God knows why." She rolled her big brown eyes. "That Zelda, she just likes to talk. Talk, talk, talk, talk, talk, but she's usually not saying nothin'. Rumor has it that Scott, her hubby, made up the term flappers because she was always flapping her gums." Then she started to laugh. "I just made that up, but it sounds good."

Willow was familiar with both women. Clara Bow was one of the biggest, if not the biggest, silent start of the 1920s. She was known for several things. She was known for her sexuality, as she slept with many men indiscriminately, including Gary Cooper for a while. She was rumored to have slept with the entire USC football team in one night, but that was just a rumor. The truth was she used to hold wild all-night parties for the team, including Marion Morrison, the football player who later became a stuntman and an actor by the name of John Wayne.

She was also known for her naïveté. She would do things like show up to a fancy dinner in a nice restaurant in a bathing suit and not understand why she was out of place. She once danced with an older gentleman who was curious about her generation and was working on an article about it. She proceeded to undress him. First, she unbuttoned his shirt and then unbuttoned his pants. As his wife was there, the older gentleman had to tell her to stop. She had no idea she was doing anything wrong.

Another thing she was known for was her refreshing lack of guile. She was the same person she always was, even after becoming famous and the biggest box office star of her time. Nothing changed her and the way she looked at the world.

Hollywood judged her because of her lack of decorum and promiscuous sex life. Clara didn't care. All she wanted was to make her movies and please her fans. She grew up in the worst slums of Brooklyn with a mother who was so mentally unbalanced that she threatened her with a butcher knife several times. This led to a lifelong battle with insomnia, as Clara was always afraid to sleep because one time she woke up and saw her mother standing over her with a butcher knife. She knew how much young girls and boys from the slums looked up to her, and she never wanted to let them down.

In the end, Clara was always looking for love. She was looking for love with all the young men that she slept with and dated. She was looking for love from her fans. She was looking for love from the people she worked with, the directors and other actors, and the people behind the scenes. She wasn't much loved by her peers - too crass, common, and wild. But she was loved by people around the world, which fed her.

As for Zelda Fitzgerald, Willow was familiar with her as well. Her upbringing was much more conventional than Clara's - she was the daughter of a prominent judge in Alabama. But she was always a wild child, the kind of girl who went to a public pool and wore a nude-colored suit that made her look naked. She and Scott were toxic to each other - they drank to excess, showed up at parties on top of taxis, got kicked out of two hotels because of their drunken behavior, and trashed every place they lived in. Scott couldn't write for years because he was too busy getting drunk and partying with Zelda. The two cheated on each other, broke up many times, and Zelda always felt neglected and unloved.

In the end, Zelda died in a mental hospital after a fire swept the place. Her mental issues might've been schizophrenia or bipolar disorder. Willow suspected the latter, as the woman was always erratic.

And now, apparently, they were haunting Willow.

And Willow had no idea why.

"Okay, out with it. Why are you here?" Willow asked Clara.

"We gotta mission. We're supposed to take you to this guy named Jackson. Guess he's your soulmate, and you seem to be turning your back on the fella. You can't do that no more. So that's where I come in," Clara explained.

Jackson. Of course. Now it was making a bit of sense. Jackson was out in Los Angeles. Clara probably was also hanging out in Los Angeles, even though she spent a few years of her life on a Nevada ranch, bringing up children and being unhappily married to an actor named Rex Bell. But she ended up back in Los Angeles, where she lived until she died.

Jackson was an actor, or trying to be. Clara was also an actor. And there was one thing that was also obvious about Clara – she really wanted to help people. Specifically, she wanted to help anybody trying to break into the movie business. She was very encouraging to men and women alike who wanted to break into the business. She was known to take several young actors under her wing to give them a shot to shine.

"And how did you manage to attach yourself to Jacqueline?" Jacquelin Delacort was a client of Willow's and had recently come to visit her for some herbal remedies. Willow somehow knew that Jacqueline had something to do with all of this, but she didn't quite know how.

Claire rolled her eyes. "That was Zelda's idea. She knew Jacqueline was coming to see you and wanted to haunt her for a little while. That Jacqueline is a real dumb bell, and that boy she's sweet on is a real dew dropper. Zelda wanted to help her see that boy was no good, but I don't think it worked."

Willow nodded her head. "Dew dropper, that means -"

"A lazy dope, that's what. She's too good for that guy, but it ain't nobody's business but hers. Anyhow, when Jacqueline came to see you, that's where we got off. We were supposed to get here anyways because this was our assignment."

Willow took a deep breath. She didn't like the sound of any of this. "Okay. Let me guess. Your assignment is to nag me into going to Los Angeles to help Jackson somehow." And then she crossed her arms. "Well, I'm here to tell you, you can nag me all you want. I'm not biting."

To that, Clara rolled her eyes. "Easy now," she said between smacks of her gum. "You don't have to marry the guy. In fact, I'm sure Zelda would tell you not to because the fella she married, he was the one who kept her down. But he needs your help."

Willow relaxed just a bit. She wasn't surprised that Zelda Fitzgerald wouldn't want her to get involved with Jackson or anybody else. Zelda was never able to get out of her husband's shadow and was never able to establish any kind of a meaningful career for herself. Even the stories she wrote for different magazines back in the day were only published because her husband had either a byline to the story, or, appallingly, were published in his name alone.

That was a shame because the lady was very talented in

many ways. She was a very talented artist and writer and was so desperate to become a prima ballerina that her inability to do so might have led to her eventual mental breakdown, although Willow suspected Zelda's heavy drinking probably was more likely to have led to her mental breakdown than anything else. And Zelda undoubtedly drank much more than she should have because her husband was a raging alcoholic, and she kept up with him.

One thing was for sure - Zelda's relationship with Scott was definitely not healthy for either of them. As for Clara, it seemed she never got close enough to any man to let them break her. She ended up broken, anyhow, but it seemed that she probably inherited her mother's mental illness. She went into a sanitarium after a mental breakdown that was possibly caused by schizophrenia, possibly caused by her mother trying to kill her with a butcher knife, or possibly caused by the lifelong insomnia she suffered because of the butcher knife incident.

Clara didn't stick around the sanitarium long enough to find out. She ended up a recluse in a bungalow, haunted by memories of a schizophrenic mother who would lock Clara in a closet while the mother turned tricks, and of a father who raped her. The doctors at the sanitarium theorized that her insomnia was related to the butcher knife incident and also because Clara was afraid that her lifelong traumas would come out in her dreams, so she was afraid to sleep.

"Clara," Willow said. "I'm not doing it. I have no desire to get involved with Jackson or any other man. Besides, he apparently needs my help to get established in Hollywood, and Hollywood was so great to you." Of course, Willow was very sarcastic when she said Hollywood was great to Clara because it obviously wasn't. She was exploited by the movie industry, not paid what she was worth and not given parts that expanded her abilities. She had no control in Hollywood.

"Hollywood saved my life, you know," Clara said. "Without the movies, I probably woulda gone crazy long before I actually did. The doctors, they thought movies were my way of escaping from my reality, and I'm sure they were. People, they thought I was a dumb bell, but I wasn't. I was just messed up in the head. You would be too if your mama was in the nut farm and your daddy messed around with you."

Willow knew this about Clara, too. She'd read her biography. She was strangely compelled to do so, even though she didn't really have an interest in the 1920s and had no desire to read about a screwed-up 1920s movie icon. Ironically, she also read Zelda's biography, even though she didn't really have an interest in her, either.

Clara read her mind. "That was me, talking in your ear. That's why you read my biography and Zelda's too. We wanted you to know what you were dealing with when we showed up."

Oh, joy. "Where's Zelda now?"

"She'll catch up. She went to her house on Long Island to see who's living there now. Zelda and me, we kind of get on each other's last nerves."

That wasn't surprising. The two women were a lot alike in too many ways. Both of them exhibitionists, both seeking attention, and both mentally ill. But Clara had accomplishments in her own name and made herself a superstar. Zelda, who didn't have any major accomplishments, probably was jealous of Clara. Zelda was always jealous of women who made their own way because she always was in the shadow of her husband.

"Listen, what if I tell you to take a hike?" Willow asked.

"You're not gonna. You gotta do this. Don't even try to say you're not gonna do it because if you do, we're never going to let you alone. We're two crazy dames, and you know I never slept when I was alive, and I don't sleep much now. You won't be able to sleep, either, because both me and Zelda, we partied all night all the time, and we'll be partying in your bedroom from now on if you don't help him."

Willow immediately thought of the movie *Ghost*, with Patrick Swayze's character, Sam Wheat, haunting Whoopi Goldberg's character, Oda Mae Brown, to force her to help his love, Molly, who was played by Demi Moore. One of the things Sam did was he didn't let Oda Mae sleep, as he sat by her bed singing "I am King Henry the Eighth I am" all night long.

She could imagine Clara and Zelda having wild parties in her bedroom while she tried to sleep. Zelda, especially, knew how to party because that's all she did. But Clara was no slouch in that department, either, as she was also famous for her all-night blowouts.

Willow realized she didn't have a choice. If she ever wanted to get rid of these two, she would have to do what they said. "Okay. What exactly do I have to do for this dude?" Willow asked.

"He needs confidence, that's all. He's in Hollywood, and he's very talented. But he's not getting a lot of roles, and he's doubting himself. He needs to know he can blow the socks off that place if he wants to, but he don't know that."

Willow finally sighed. "Okay. As long as you're not trying to force me into a relationship with the guy, I guess I'll have to go along. I don't like it, but I really don't like the idea of you guys haunting me with your all-night parties every night of my life. I need my beauty rest."

Clara rolled her eyes and smacked her gum. "I never

slept. Not really. You don't need no rest, either. That's all they ever say, you gotta get your sleep. I'm here to tell you sleep is overrated. But, okay, as long as you come with us, we'll let you get your shut-eye."

And then Clara looked behind her. "Nice of you to show up, Zelda. Late as usual."

"You're a fine one to talk," Zelda Fitzgerald said to Clara.

"Listen, Toots, I made almost 60 movies in just a few years, and I was never late to the set. You never had to be nowhere. Maybe that's why you're always late now. You never had no place to be, so no way were you ever late nowhere. But you got places to be now, so you better be on time next time."

Zelda's face, such as it was, turned bright red. "She's always rubbing it in that she was a major star and I was a nobody," Zelda said to Willow.

Clara just cocked her head a little bit. "I know I bust her chops. I don't know why. I was never like that when I was alive. I never wanted to hurt no one's feelings. But Zelda, you just rub me the wrong way."

"Likewise."

Willow just looked at Zelda. Clara obviously wasn't going to take "no" for an answer, but maybe Zelda would listen to reason. "Zelda, I don't know why you and Clara so want me to help Jackson in his movie career. You and Scott didn't exactly have a great relationship in Hollywood. You know how superficial and ridiculous the place is. So why do you want me to help him so much?"

"Scott had a problem in Hollywood because he felt that writing scripts were beneath him," Zelda said. "He felt everything was beneath him, except for his novels. He was really full of himself. But that had nothing to do with me. I didn't care about being out in Hollywood, or anywhere else, for that matter. Because everywhere we went, our problems followed us, so it didn't matter if we lived in Hollywood, the south of France, Connecticut, Long Island, St. Paul, Alabama, or New York. Wherever we went, the drinking and the parties never stopped, Scott never paid attention to me, and I always felt like a failure. Hollywood was a place where I felt like an insignificant little bug, but that was true for every place I lived."

"Yeah," Clara said. "Wherever you go, there you are."

"Clara, do you think Hollywood is a place for Jackson?"

"I told ya, Hollywood was the place where I wasn't crazy. I only went loony when I left the place. Jackson, I visited him, and he's a pretty good bird. Besides, he's the bee's knees. Dreamy. And he don't have no screw loose. He's a good egg, and that's the truth. He'll do fine."

Willow finally just took a deep breath. "Well, it looks like I'm going to Hollywood."

Clara just smiled and cracked her gum. "I knew ya'd come around."

The Beachfront Sunsets: Chapter Three

Willow

The only thing for Willow to do before going to Hollywood was she had to tell Hallie what she was doing. After all, Hallie would have to hold down the fort for her while she was in California.

She explained the situation, and Hallie, perhaps not surprisingly, took it all in stride. Hallie knew, as everybody did, that Willow sometimes was haunted by ghosts she could see and hear. That was part of the curse of being sensitive and able to see beyond the veil. And, yes, she considered the ability to see and hear spirits to be a curse, not a blessing. Normal people didn't have to put up with a ghost's demands, lest they have to put up with all-night parties if they didn't do what the ghosts wanted.

"But, boy, that's fascinating for you," Hallie said with raised eyebrows. "You're going to be hanging out with the biggest silent star of the 1920s and the wife of F. Scott Fitzgerald? Color me green with envy."

Willow didn't really see it that way. To her, these two ghosts, and every ghost who had haunted her because she was supposed to do something for somebody, were nothing but a pain in the ass. She hated being directed by anybody, let alone by a being who could make her life a living hell. And one thing was for sure, Clara Bow and Zelda Fitzgerald knew about making people's lives a living hell.

"Hallie, I wish you'd have my life for just a day. If you did, you wouldn't think this was so cool. And now I have to go to Los Angeles."

Hallie nodded her head. "You're going to be helping Jackson, then?"

"Yes. For whatever reason, he needs confidence." Willow thought about the irony that she was just telling Jacqueline that she could do a spell for her to make her more of a badass. Jackson apparently needed that for himself. There was nothing else she could really do for him. It wasn't in her wheelhouse to perform a spell to get him a job, so she just had to burn some candles, gather some herbs, light some sage, chant some words, and hope that all did the trick.

After that, she was going to be done. Done with Jackson, done with Los Angeles, and hopefully done with Clara Bow and Zelda Fitzgerald.

Just then, Ava came in the door with a bouquet of wild-flowers. "My son sent this to me," she said with a look of wonder on her face. "And something told me to bring them over here for your spa because I don't think they're for me so much as I think they're for Willow. Don't ask me why I think that."

Willow looked at the bouquet, with the pink, purple, and white peonies mixed in with sunflowers and lilacs real-ized that Ava was probably correct. Peonies, sunflowers, and lilacs were her favorite flowers. She was never much of a rose girl - she always liked the flowers she could find in a field growing wild. Jackson probably meant for the bouquet to come to her because he probably had a feeling that Willow was going to be out to see him soon to help him. Not that she'd called Jackson or even told Ava what she was about to do.

"Thanks for bringing that bouquet over, Ava," Willow said. "These will look beautiful at the front desk."

Ava looked slightly dazed. "Yeah, like I said, it's really weird for my son to send me something like this. He's not a flower kind of guy, to say the very least. Anyhow, enjoy them."

"I'd like to say I'll enjoy them, but I'm not going to probably. I'm going to Los Angeles, and I don't know when I'll be back."

Hallie had a huge grin on her face. "Can I tell Ava what's going on?" she asked eagerly.

"Sure, why not?" Willow asked. "Ava might as well know about my freaky experiences too."

"Willow is now friends with Clara Bow and Zelda Fitzgerald," she said to Ava.

"Clara Bow and Zelda Fitzgerald? You mean two women who have been dead for a long time?" Ava asked.

"Yeah, isn't that exciting?" Hallie asked. "And she's going to go out to help Jackson. That's probably why he sent the flowers. He somehow knew Willow was coming out there to see him."

Ava gave Willow a strange look. "You know, I'm surprised, but not really. Why are those ghosts coming to see you?"

"Hell, I don't know why they've been assigned this wonderful thing to do to me. I only know I have to do it, or else they'll haunt me by having wild parties in my bedroom every night. And, trust me, those two girls knew how to party."

Ava took a deep breath and smiled. "You know, I'm really happy you're going to help Jackson. He really needs a boost of confidence. He's very talented, but so is every Tom, Dick, and Harry out in Los Angeles trying to get a leg up in the movie industry. He's just one more pretty face in a sea of them."

Just then, Clara Bow showed up. "Hiya, Toots," she said in her usual greeting. "You gotta get a wiggle on. Jackson gotta audition next week, and he don't think he's gotta shot. It's a big part, and you gotta give him that boost that he can do it. It's important because he's just hanging around his place, feeling sorry for himself and drinking foot juice."

"Foot juice?" Willow asked her. "What does that mean?"

"Hooch, giggle water, cheap wine," Clara said. "He's getting zozzled every night instead of studying lines. You know what, now that I think about it, that's probably why Zelda hooked me up on this. Her husband, he got blotto all the time instead of writing, and it ruined him. You're supposed to stop Jackson from doing that to himself."

Willow turned back to Hallie and Ava, who were looking at her curiously. "Yes, Clara Bow is here in this room right now. She was just telling me that your son is drinking too much. And I guess he has a big audition next week he's going to blow if he doesn't get some confidence in himself."

"And he won't get that role if he don't quit getting so soused every night," Clara said with a nod of her fire engine red head. "So come on, we gotta get going lickety-split."

Willow just raised her eyebrows and shook her head. "The things I have to put up with. I wish I wasn't born with these gifts. To say my life would be much simpler if I could just tell women like Clara Bow to take a hike and leave me alone would be an understatement."

To that, Clara took her thumb and hiked it towards the door. "Come on, don't just sit there like some kind of dumb bell. That boy knows his onions, that's for sure, but he don't know he knows his onions. That's where you come in."

"Knows his onions?" Willow asked. She would have to brush up on her 20's slang if she was going to keep up with this woman.

"He knows his stuff," Clara said. "He's really good. You have to help him see that."

Ava was wringing her hands. "Jackson is drinking a lot? That doesn't sound like him."

Just then, Zelda appeared. "I was trying to figure out why I got this assignment, but now I understand. If your man is drinking too much, and the sauce is keeping him from fulfilling his potential, then it's important that I'm involved in helping you prevent that from happening." She appeared to sigh. "I could never stop Scott from drinking. And if he wasn't drinking so much, he could've been known as the greatest writer that ever lived. Look at Ernest Hemingway - he won a Nobel Prize for literature and a Pulitzer Prize for *The Old Man and the Sea*. That should've been Scott."

Clara shook her head. "That Ernest Hemingway, he wasn't exactly dry himself. He tied one on a lot, too. But he didn't have no anchor bringing him down like Scott had. If a dame became a ball and chain for him, he just cut 'em loose."

Zelda narrowed her eyes at Clara. "I'm sick and tired of you implying that I was the reason why Scott didn't achieve his potential. As I see it, *he* was why *I* didn't attain *my* potential."

"Let's face it, you two were poison to each other," Clara said. "It would've been better if the two of you never met."

"I agree with that," Zelda said. "At any rate, I know about the sauce cutting short what you're supposed to achieve. And I've been assigned many cases where people are drinking too much when they're supposed to focus on their dreams. I don't know why I keep getting these hard-luck cases. It's like I have to keep living my nightmare over and over again. Oh, well."

Willow turned to Ava. "Yes, apparently, Jackson is drinking too much. I'm sorry to tell you that."

Ava just shook her head. "I don't like the sound of that. Jackson has always been so levelheaded. So cool about everything. But I wonder if he keeps it all bottled in. I've always thought that might be the case. I've always worried about him because I can never get into his head to see how he's feeling. He always just tells me not to worry. But now, that's what I'm going to be doing – worrying."

"Tell your buddy it's applesauce for her to worry," Clara said between the smacks of her gum.

Zelda rolled her eyes. "Clara, you have to stop using so many slang words. Nobody's going to know what you're talking about."

"Like you're so high-falutin you never used no slang," Clara shot back. "You think you're such a cupcake, but you're not."

Zelda shook her head. "Applesauce means nonsense, just in case you're wondering."

Willow was wondering that, but she got the gist of it from the context. "Ava, let me just put your mind at ease. I'm going out to give Jackson a confidence boost. And if I do, he'll get the big part he's going for next week. At least, that's kind of what I'm getting from these two bickering ghosts."

"That's right, you'll tell Jackson he can do it, and he'll believe you. And it's his destiny to get this part, so that's why we have to help you help him," Zelda said.

"Sarah's going out to Los Angeles too," Ava said. "I worry about her. She finally fell in love with somebody good, or at least he seems to be, but he doesn't have long to live. So he's going out to stay with his sister in Los Angeles to get residency there and die with dignity. I can't imagine what Sarah's going through right now. Maybe after you help Jackson, you can help Sarah get past the grief she'll feel after she goes through that."

Willow wasn't aware that this was happening to Sarah. She wasn't a part of the inner circle, even though she was pretty good friends with Hallie. Hallie hadn't told her the story of Sarah and her new beau.

But somehow, Willow knew Sarah was going to be okay. "She's going to be a new mother," Willow said. "That's what I'm getting about the situation with your sister Sarah. That's been her lifelong dream, to be a mother. I think she's going to be just fine."

Ava nodded her head. "Yeah, actually. Sarah accidentally married Max. Well, it wasn't really accidental, but it definitely wasn't something she did sober. But she'll be a stepmother to Max's daughter, Julia, after Max passes away. I'd ask you how you knew that, but I already know the answer to that question."

"Yeah, it's a curse. Definitely."

Clara and Zelda were now standing at the doorway, looking at Willow like they both wanted her to run out the door. "Get your plane booked and let's get out of here," Clara said. "Let's get that bird in the air."

"Okay. I'm coming, I'm coming," Willow said. "Okay, ladies, I'll see you when I get back. Whenever that's going to be. Hallie, I trust you to hold down the fort while I'm gone. Of course, we're not going to be able to book anybody for acupuncture or herbal treatments or chakra balancing or any of that, so this whole thing will cost me a pretty penny."

"Oh, cry me a river," Clara said. "You'll make the money back when you do what you're supposed to do with your fella. Now, move."

At that, Willow followed Clara and Zelda out the door.

"At least let me take you to the airport," Ava said to Willow. "If you're going to be helping my son, that's the least I can do for you."

So, Willow followed Ava into her car so that Ava could drive her to the airport. She booked a plane ticket on the way. "I'm just booking a plane ticket for myself," Willow pointedly said to Clara and Zelda. "You girls can find your own way out there."

"Don't worry, we will. Now come on, let's scram," Clara said.

Grab your copy...
vinci-books.com/beachfront-sunsets

About the Author

Ainsley Keaton lives with her hubby and two fur-babies in Southern California. When she's not binge-watching *Grace and Frankie*, *Succession* and *Downton Abbey*, she's reading historical and women's fiction and scouring the beach for sea glass and sand dollars.